INITIATION BY DESIRE

What Reviewers Say About MJ Williamz's Work

"*Forbidden Passions* is hot, hot, hot. …A well-written story with a good mix of history and erotica, *Forbidden Passions* will surely ignite the passion within yourself!"—*Bibliographic Book Blog*

"MJ Williamz, in her first romantic thriller, has done an impressive job of building up the tension and suspense. *Shots Fired* clearly shows the author's ability to spin an engaging tale and is sure to be just the beginning of great things to follow as the author moves forward."—*Lambda Literary*

"*Forbidden Passions* is 192 pages of bodice ripping antebellum erotica not so gently wrapped in the moistest, muskiest pantalets of lesbian horn dog high jinks ever written. …*Forbidden Passions* is the very model of modern major erotica, but hidden within the sweet swells and trembling clefts of that erotica is a beautiful May-September romance between two wonderful and memorable characters. M.J. Williamz has a wide reputation for her short stories, and has now given her fans a sound and playful second novel." —*Rainbow Reader*

In *Shots Fired*…"Williamz keeps the reader guessing and turning the pages to get to the bottom of the mystery."—*Story Circle Book Reviews*

Visit us at www.boldstrokesbooks.com

By the Author

Initiation by Desire

Forbidden Passions

Shots Fired

INITIATION BY DESIRE

by

MJ Williamz

2012

INITIATION BY DESIRE

© 2012 By MJ Williamz. All Rights Reserved.

ISBN 10: 1-60282-590-4
ISBN 13: 978-1-60282-590-1

This Trade Paperback Original Is Published By
Bold Strokes Books, Inc.
P.O. Box 249
Valley Falls, NY 12185

First Edition: January 2012

THIS IS A WORK OF FICTION. NAMES, CHARACTERS, PLACES, AND INCIDENTS ARE THE PRODUCT OF THE AUTHOR'S IMAGINATION OR ARE USED FICTITIOUSLY. ANY RESEMBLANCE TO ACTUAL PERSONS, LIVING OR DEAD, BUSINESS ESTABLISHMENTS, EVENTS, OR LOCALES IS ENTIRELY COINCIDENTAL.

THIS BOOK, OR PARTS THEREOF, MAY NOT BE REPRODUCED IN ANY FORM WITHOUT PERMISSION.

CREDITS
EDITOR: CINDY CRESAP
PRODUCTION DESIGN: SUSAN RAMUNDO
COVER DESIGN BY SHERI (GRAPHICARTIST2020@HOTMAIL.COM)

Acknowledgments

As always, first thank-yous go to my son for always believing in me and doing his level best to keep me on task when I'm writing. Next, my sincere gratitude again to ABR for taking the time to beta this book for me. And for the years of support and encouragement she's given me. Last, but not least, huge thank-yous to Cindy Cresap for her patience during the edits and rewrites and Rad for once again giving me the opportunity to share my writing with the world.

Dedication

For Bremer, without whom I never would have
survived my own college years

CHAPTER ONE

Sue Dobson strained against the black silk scarves that bound her to the bedposts. Her head thrashed wildly on the steel gray pillow as her hips rose to greet each thrust of the nine-inch latex cock being drilled into her.

"Oh, God, that's it, Mel. Fuck me. Please fuck me."

She moaned as Mel bit and sucked her hard nipple while she plunged the dildo deeper with each thrust of her hips, then slowly dragged its length over her turgid clit as she pulled it out.

"Are you close?" Mel whispered hoarsely. "I can't hold out much longer."

"I'm ready," Sue moaned. She wrapped her legs around Mel's waist and ground into the base of the tool while Mel pressed back as hard as she could. She gyrated against Mel, lost in the feelings that had begun between her legs and were now taking over her body.

She heard Mel cry out at the same time she did, the orgasms perfectly timed after so many similar encounters over the years.

Mel collapsed on top of Sue, leaving her cock still buried.

"Holy fuck, Mel. That was one of the best."

"Yeah, it was. I could do this all night."

"Don't start, Mel," Sue said.

Mel rolled off her, abruptly breaking their connection. Lying on her back, she turned to Sue. "You can't blame me for trying. We've been doing this off and on thing for how long? The sex is great. But I keep thinking that maybe, just once, you'll spend the night and I can see how many orgasms I can coax out of you in a twelve-hour period."

"Untie me."

Mel grinned at her. "And if I don't?"

"Very funny." Sue felt fear clenching her stomach. She hadn't considered for a second that Mel wouldn't release her after playtime. "Seriously. Let me go."

As Sue lay there, Mel moved back on top of her, resting her cock against Sue's pussy, the leather of her harness all that was separating their skin.

"I think I want you to stay." She nibbled Sue's neck.

"I can't and you know that." Sue tried to sound more playful than she felt.

"You sure?" Mel asked, kissing lower.

"I'm sure." She looked over Mel's shoulder at the clock. "I have to be home in half an hour. You need to untie me and save some of those hormones for the next time we run into each other at the bar."

Mel let out a long sigh before reaching up and untying her.

Sue held back a moan as the dildo pressed against her. As much as she wanted more, she had responsibilities and needed to get home.

Sue was aware of Mel's focus on her as she hurriedly dressed. "Is your home situation ever going to change?" Mel asked.

"Of course. I just don't know when."

"Might it be any time soon?"

"It might. It might not. Believe me, you'll be one of the first to know." Sue kissed her good-bye and saw herself out.

❖

"Stand closer together," Piper Abrams, Pledge Master of the Gamma Alpha Epsilons, commanded. "I want shoulders touching. Closer!"

The fifteen young coeds, clad only in their panties and bras, moved sideways, eager to make their pledge mistress happy and end the long night.

Nineteen-year-old Tulley Stephens's stomach roiled. She hated touching. The feel of the other girls' skin pressing against hers made her uncomfortable. She already felt out of place. Her white boxer briefs and sports bra made her stand out among the others in their silky, French-cut panties and flimsy, barely-there bras.

The concrete floor of the basement was hard and cold on her bare feet, but her humiliation and discomfort kept her warm. Even so, she could feel her nipples poking at her bra and felt exposed to the group of active sorority members sitting behind the pledge mistress.

"Your line looks like shit!" the pledge mistress yelled again. "Can't you ladies do anything right? Work as a team, damn it. Keep your shoulders touching and straighten out that line."

The pledges looked at one another down the line and moved until they were certain they were standing in a straight line.

"Is that the best you can do?"

The girls began to adjust the line again.

"Did I tell you to move? I asked you a simple question." She enunciated each word. "Is that the best you can do?"

"Yes," they mumbled.

"What?"

"Yes, ma'am!"

"I want to hear you say it in one voice. Jesus Christ, you're a pathetic group. I don't think you'll ever be able to act as one. It's not that hard. And if you don't get it right soon, none of you will ever be initiated."

"Yes, ma'am!" they yelled again in unison.

The room was silent as Piper stood there, hands on hips, surveying the line in front of her. She turned to her sisters behind her. "Do we want to subject ourselves to their incompetence anymore tonight?"

The active members talked among themselves and sounded dejected as they told her no, they couldn't take any more disappointment. She faced the pledges again.

"Fine. It's bedtime. Get your sleeping bags out of the corner and carry them upstairs. You'll sleep in the game room. Now go."

The pledges grabbed their sleeping bags and got back in a line. Turning, they followed one another up the stairs and through the house to the game room, maintaining the line the whole time.

Tulley groaned internally when she saw the four large fans arranged in the fourteen-by-sixteen-foot room. When they were all inside standing between the pool and foosball tables that had been pushed against the wall, the pledge mistress cut through them.

"These fans will be on high all night. They'd better be on when we wake you up in the morning. You'll sleep in your underwear. All night. When we come in tomorrow, if anyone is wearing more, we'll tag another week to your pledge period. Is this understood?"

"Yes, ma'am," they said as one.

As soon as the door was closed, they relaxed and started to chatter. They chose their sleeping areas and rolled out their bags. Tulley laid hers against one wall, under a pool table, hoping to stay as far out of the way of the fans as possible. The air-conditioner in the house was already on high, which she was sure was for their benefit.

The warmth of her sleeping bag offered immediate relief as she slid in and lay on her back, arms folded under her head, and stared at the filthy underside of the pool table. She asked herself why she had ever allowed her mother to talk her into pledging a sorority. She clearly didn't belong. But she also knew she was still trying to win her mother's approval, and if this was how it was to happen, then so be it.

Besides, her first year at Fenton State had been rough. She hadn't connected with anyone either from the dorms or in her classes, so she didn't have any real friends at school. She was determined to break out of her shell and meet people, and her mother's suggestion to join a sorority was logical in that regard. But she didn't feel the bond the others seemed to feel. She took a deep breath and told herself, yet again, to give it some time. Pledging was almost over. Maybe things would change when she became an active member.

The chatter had quieted down as the girls settled in to sleep. Tulley rolled onto her side and closed her eyes. She was beginning to drift when she heard someone complain, "I'm cold."

Another disembodied voice said, "Courtney? Is that you?"

"Yes. It's freezing in here."

"Well, come over here. You can slide into my sleeping bag. We'll keep each other warm."

Tulley's heart skipped a beat. That was just wrong. Soon sounds of sleeping bags unzipping and zipping filled the room. Tulley lay there hoping no one wanted to share hers. She was starting to relax again when there was giggling from the girls next to her.

"Watch where your hands are," she heard.

"Oh, you loved it." She heard more giggles.

"You're just lucky I don't sleep in the nude," one joked.

"Or maybe I'm not so lucky."

Tulley didn't move. She wanted to cover her ears but didn't want to rustle the bag and bring attention to herself. How could these girls even joke like that? She was less comfortable than she had ever been in her entire life. The idea of leaving the sorority house right then and forgetting all this nonsense crossed her mind.

Instead, she made herself lie in place and listen as quiet eventually filled the room once again. The temperature had dropped, so she pulled her sleeping bag close around her and waited for sleep to take her away from the nightmare she was living.

❖

The parking area was well lit as Sue maneuvered her green Subaru Impreza into the space reserved for her. It was a few minutes before two a.m., so she would be able to sneak in before her curfew. She was aware, deep down, that missing the curfew she'd agreed to when she took the position of RA wouldn't be the end of the world. Not even close, but she liked to use it as an excuse to avoid spending the night anywhere. She liked to keep her relationships commitment free, and she didn't want to give any woman false hope.

Knowing some of her charges might still be up, she carefully opened the back door and tiptoed down the hall. Her room was across from the kitchen, which was often the meeting point at that hour on the weekend, with everyone exchanging stories of their evenings. Tonight had not been the norm, though, so the kitchen was empty, allowing Sue to slip unnoticed to her room.

She rubbed at the slight red marks around her wrists as she undressed and smiled as she relived the sensations Mel brought to her. She and Mel had been sleeping together for close to four years. They first ran into each other at the only lesbian bar in town about a year after Sue moved back from Novato when she decided she wanted to go to graduate school. Neither of them was a commitment kind of woman, so it suited them fine to get together for sex whenever they happened to be at the bar alone. They were nowhere near girlfriends, more like fuck buddies. And it suited each of them just fine. Even if Mel did pester Sue to spend the night more often than she'd like.

Slipping under the covers, Sue wondered again if it was time to give up her position with the sorority and get a place of her own where she could come and go as she pleased. She knew that wasn't feasible, though. She was a struggling grad student, and the room and board the sorority provided spared her from having to work while she was in school. Besides, she couldn't complain about the few responsibilities she had over her charges. Still, sometimes she wondered if it might be time to grow up and move out on her own.

She dismissed those questions and allowed memories of Mel's face dancing above hers to be the last thing she saw as she fell fast asleep.

❖

Sue's internal clock went off at six o'clock the next morning and she stretched, wishing just once she was able to sleep in like normal people. She heard voices coming from the kitchen and remembered what special day had dawned.

She waved at the women seated around the long table in the corner as she helped herself to a cup of coffee. Starting to feel more alert, she walked down the hall toward the game room. She peeked in at all the sleeping women and smiled at the sight of them two to a sleeping bag. She could imagine the feel of their soft, smooth skin pressed against each other, body heat seeping from one to the other.

Her own pledge period had been similar. The rituals had been the same for many years. And the night before her pledging ended six years earlier, she too had slept in the game room in her underwear with fans blowing unyieldingly on her sisters and her. Sue was still grateful Tabitha Wilson had been in her pledge class. Tabitha was also a lesbian. Although she later broke Sue's heart by refusing to continue their affair and by pretending to be straight to fit in, that night of pledge week when they shared a sleeping bag had been almost heaven.

Sue allowed herself a moment of pleasant recall.

Tabitha had climbed into her sleeping bag as the other pledges were doubling up in search of warmth. She and Tabitha had flirted clandestinely most of the semester, and one night after a party, they had retreated to Sue's dorm room and spent the night finally giving in to their desires, exploring each other's body and sharing pleasures that continued until morning.

But that night at the sorority house, once Tabitha was in her bag, Sue had immediately caressed her breast as their mouths met in a hungry kiss. Sue pushed Tabitha's bra up and moaned as she felt the soft, supple flesh. She teased the nipple for a moment before sliding her hand down Tab's taut stomach and running her fingers over her damp satin panties.

Her ministrations stopped when she felt Tabitha's hand close around her wrist.

"What?" Sue whispered.

"No."

"Why?"

"Are you crazy? We're in the middle of a room full of our pledge sisters."

"We'll just have to be quiet." Sue tried to break free of Tab's grip.

"I said no. I'm not going to take that chance."

"I can't believe you're doing this to me." Sue moved her arm so the back of Tabitha's hand pressed against her own crotch, which was drenched with need.

With a low groan, Tab pulled their hands away.

"We can't do this here."

Sue slid down and pulled the sleeping bag over their heads. She kissed Tabitha with every bit of pent up passion she was feeling. Her kiss was returned in kind, and she rolled on top of Tab, grinding her hips into her. She thought Tab was crazy not wanting to take advantage of the situation, when she heard giggling coming from another sleeping bag. She slipped off Tabitha and rolled her over, spooning against her.

"I wonder what's going on over there," she whispered in Tab's ear.

"I think you know, and I'm glad you see my point."

"Heck yeah, I do. Now let's get some sleep."

The memory of Tabitha's soft, warm body in her arms was so real she was startled when Piper tapped her on the shoulder. She forced her thoughts back to the present and away from the frustrating and painful memories of days gone by.

"Hey, Sue. It's time we wake them up."

"Oh, yes. Sorry." Sue moved out of their way and let the active members in to wake the exhausted pledges. She made her way to her room to get ready for the day. She had little to do with the pledges, but she had to stay in the house all day in case anything went wrong. She planned to stay in her room until the house had emptied so, if needed, she could say she didn't know which way the group went when they left the house. The need hadn't arisen before, but she knew enough to cover her ass.

❖

Tulley grimaced at the sound of pots and pans being rattled by her head. She had no idea what time it was but knew it was way too early to be up on a Saturday. Especially since she assumed they had been kept up late the night before. The prior afternoon, they had been required to turn in their watches, cell phones, PDAs, anything that would display time. They were at the mercy of the active chapter, Piper in particular. She knew it was to teach them trust, but she felt that could be accomplished without all the condescension.

They dressed quickly and marched to the kitchen, where they enjoyed a breakfast of pancakes and bacon. As soon as breakfast was over, they were ordered to brush their teeth and form a straight line on the sidewalk in front of the old Victorian house.

"Form a line! A real line! A straight line! Shoulders touching!" Piper yelled.

The pledges repeated their actions of the previous night. They bunched together and straightened their line.

One of the actives opened the back doors of a black van and ordered the girls to get in and sit down. She handed each a black blindfold as they climbed in.

"Put those on and keep them on. Do not take them off until I tell you. Is that understood?"

"Yes, ma'am," they said in unison.

When the van was full, Piper climbed in and closed the door behind her.

Tulley sat quietly as the van took off. It felt like they were driving in circles. She did her best to follow where they might be going but soon gave up and let the rolling motion of the van lull her to sleep.

The van stopped abruptly, jarring Tulley from a pleasant dream where she was still a young girl running through her father's vineyards in Ukiah.

"Take your blindfolds off, but I want eyes on the floor. No looking out the window," Piper's voice cut through the silence.

The pledges did as they were instructed, and Tulley fought the urge to look out the tinted windows to see where they were and what all the activity was outside. Bright light burst in as the back doors were opened abruptly. Tulley squinted in pain.

"Get out orderly and carefully. When you're out, form a line facing the cars. Understood?"

"Yes, ma'am." They were still in unison, but the enthusiasm was obviously waning.

When the girls were out and lined up, Piper once again took her place in front of the actives who were lined up in front of several cars parked in the middle of an orchard. On the ground in front of the pledges were three thick leather belts and five milk jugs. Tulley had no guess what would happen to them now.

"Each of those milk jugs holds a gallon of water. You will need it. Don't be greedy and drink it all in the beginning or you'll be very sorry later." She paused to let the tidbit of information sink in. And, it seemed, hopefully confuse and scare them.

"You need to walk home from here. You will be back at the house by noon. That's not a suggested time. You will be there by then. Understood?"

Tulley held her breath, hoping none of her pledge sisters would be stupid enough to point out their lack of time-telling devices. No one said a thing.

Together they replied, "Yes, ma'am."

They stood silently and closed their eyes against the dust kicked up by the actives' cars as they drove off, leaving the pledges to work together to accomplish their latest task.

CHAPTER TWO

The grumbling began before the dust settled.

"Back to the house by noon? How are we supposed to know what time it is?"

"Where are we? It seems like we were driving forever."

"We were," Tulley said. "But I know in the beginning we weren't really going anywhere. We were just driving around a block or two."

"I thought that, too," a short, spunky girl named Livie added.

"Okay, it's about eight thirty," Tulley said.

"How do you know?" someone whined.

"The sun," she said. "Didn't any of you ever go camping and have to tell time by the sun?"

She stared at the blank faces.

"Are you serious?" Danielle, a typical blond daddy's girl who would soon be a sorority girl, sneered. She was every stereotype Tulley couldn't stand. But without the active members yelling at them to work as a team, Danielle ignored her.

"So three and a half hours to get back to the house? But we have no idea how far away the house is." Livie brushed her bangs out of her eyes.

"You guys are forgetting I grew up here," Kelly, another blonde, pointed out.

"Still." Danielle looked every bit the bitch she was. "All these orchards look the same. So the fact that you're a local isn't much help."

Tulley stood looking at her pledge class, dressed in their mulberry and sterling pledge jerseys, and noticed they had split into two groups. Eight of them were standing with Danielle, arms crossed, looking bored and disgusted. The other five were standing with her, looking between her and Danielle.

"They don't necessarily all look the same," Kelly said. "There's something about this place that looks familiar."

Danielle rolled her eyes, but Tulley turned her attention to Kelly. "How so?"

"Well, this clearing, for example. Most farmers pack as many almond trees as possible into every orchard. They wouldn't leave this opening here."

"Please," Danielle said. "I wouldn't exactly call this a clearing."

"Yes, it is. If those six cars and the van parked here, it's a clearing. Besides, they could easily have planted another three or four trees here," Kelly said.

"Is there anything else?" Livie asked, not sounding totally convinced either.

Kelly turned in place and surveyed the orchard around her. She pointed to an old, dilapidated metal building and laughed. "Yes! I know where we are. We're at the Davidsons'. We used to have keggers in that outbuilding."

"Excellent. So now that we know where we are, how far away is the house?" Tulley asked.

"Not that far, really. We just need to get to Cascade Street, the main artery from the ag zone to the city, and follow it to town. I'd guess it'll take us a couple hours to get there."

"Okay, so let's get started." Tulley grabbed a long leather belt and slid it through her belt loops. She slipped a milk jug on it, knotted it off, and slipped another one on. She looped the belt through that, then slipped one more jug on, knotted it off and finally slid the tongue end of the belt through the last loop. She buckled the belt tightly and checked that she she'd evenly distributed the weight of the water.

Though she was average height and weight at five seven and one hundred fifty pounds, she was fit and strong from working whenever necessary on her parents' vineyard back home.

She turned to the rest of the group. "Come on. There's only two bottles left. One of you carry one and one carry the other. We can alternate as we go. But we need to get going, so come on."

Tulley looked at Kelly. "Lead the way to Cascade."

They walked together through the orchard, Tulley never questioning Kelly. Livie walked behind them with a jug of water strapped to her waist. The other group was still at the clearing, arguing over who had to carry the last jug.

"I sure hope this pledge period ends soon, so we can quit associating with them," Livie said.

"My understanding is we're sisters for life or some crap," Tulley said snidely.

Her friends laughed at her.

"Lucky us," Livie said.

Tulley turned to see the other group walking slowly toward them.

"Okay," she told her contingency, "we need to wait for them."

To the others, she called, "Come on. We need to walk as a group. And thanks, Michelle, for carrying that last water."

They didn't pick up their pace but finally caught up.

"Why do we have to be a group out here?" Danielle asked, looking like she'd rather do just about anything than associate with them.

"Do you really think they're going to leave us alone the whole walk back to the house? Do you feel like having someone drive by and yell at us for not being a team? Because I'm getting pretty tired of being yelled at, myself."

"Whatever." Danielle looked at Kelly. "Just get us back to the house."

Tulley resisted the urge to slap her. Instead, she told herself that anything else the actives did to them as pledges couldn't be as bad as being stuck in the middle of nowhere with Danielle.

In silence, the group followed Kelly through the orchard until they reached a two-lane road.

"This is Cascade," she said. "We just follow it east until it reaches Lassen."

"Oh, yeah," Livie piped up. "Lassen and Cascade is where the park is. That's only a few blocks from the house."

Their sorority house was at Lassen and Walnut, five blocks south of Cascade. A murmur of hope worked its way through the group.

They had walked about a quarter of a mile when Livie sang out, "I don't know, but I've been told."

The rest answered less enthusiastically, "I don't know but I've been told."

"G-A-Es are good as gold!"

"G-A-Es are good as gold."

"Sound off!" Livie called out.

"One, two."

"Say it again."

"Three, four."

"Bring it on down."

In unison, the group shouted, "One, two, three, four, one, two… three, four!"

A few clapped and cheered, making Tulley's skin crawl. She had never liked cheerleaders and hated having to act like one. The fact that these girls actually enjoyed it made her question her decision to pledge yet again. She chastised herself to stop finding fault with everything and focus on the good that would come out of the sorority. She knew she was stressed and on edge from Hell Week. She cleared her mind of the negativity and walked on.

Livie continued leading cheers as they walked, the April sun beating down on them. When Tulley estimated they had been walking for an hour, she called everyone to a halt.

"We need to take a break," she said. "Let's sit under some trees and drink a little water."

The group sat in an orchard that bordered the road and leaned against trees as Tulley passed around one of the jugs of water.

"Don't drink too much," she said, "we don't need anyone cramping up out here."

They were quiet as they rested, enjoying the water and shade.

"This water's not cold," one of Danielle's group complained.

"Imagine that," Tulley said. "I've been carrying it in the heat and it's not cold."

There was a smattering of snickers that quickly died down when a car slowed as it drove by, yelling at them.

"You lazy pledges! Get up and get marching. You'll never make it to the house on time."

The van from earlier drove up behind the car. The passenger rolled down her window. "If any of you wants a ride, come on. We'll give you one."

Tulley and Danielle glared at the group. Tulley knew there would be hell to pay if any pledge broke from the unit. She waved to the van. "We're good. Thanks."

As the van sped off, she stood and addressed the group. "We need to get going. I want Livie and Michelle to pass off their water jugs to someone else to carry. I can keep mine for now. Get that done and we'll hit the road."

They continued along their way with Livie leading more Gamma Alpha Epsilon songs. The girls repeated one particularly annoying one for so long Tulley finally broke down and joined in.

"Ooh, ooh, I'm glad I'm a G-A-E. Ooh, ooh, I'm glad I'm a G-A-E. Ooh, ooh, I'm glad I'm a G-A-E. It's G-A-E for me!"

Their journey continued on, with frequent stops for shade and water, until they reached the park at Cascade and Lassen. Tulley checked the position of the sun. It was eleven thirty.

"I think we have time for a quick break. Let's sit at a picnic table for a few minutes to catch our breath. That way, we'll be better prepared for whatever they have planned for us when we get back."

They rested for ten minutes before Tulley roused them up and into a line. The column moved down Lassen until they reached the Gamma Alpha Epsilon house. They formed a line, shoulder to shoulder, and stood on the sidewalk in front.

The pledges started singing another song when the door opened and Piper came out to the covered cement porch and stood looking at them. She slowly walked down the steps while the rest of the actives made their way out to join her.

Piper stared at the line of women. Tulley was surprised to feel her heart race slightly. She hadn't realized how much she dreaded the rest of the day.

"Go into the game room," Piper said, then stepped aside as they filed past.

They sat restlessly at first, chattering among themselves as they wondered what could possibly be next. The room grew quiet as the wait grew longer and their morning hike took its toll.

"I'm tired," Kelly said. "You think we'll be in here long enough to take a nap?"

"Go for it," Livie told her. "I'll cover for you."

Tulley had no idea how long they'd been in there. Kelly was snoring slightly when Piper came in to get them.

"Everybody up. Now. Get to the sidewalk and form a line."

The pledges scrambled to their feet, with Livie and Tulley trying to rouse Kelly without being noticed. She was a little groggy but managed to make it outside with the two of them holding on to her. The line was formed quickly, every girl's shoulder touching another's. To their surprise, Piper said nothing about straightening the line. She did, however, point to the same van they'd ridden in that morning.

"Everyone turn to their right. Stay in line and walk to the van."

They did as they were told and dutifully took the blindfolds they were handed as they climbed in.

Tulley's stomach was in knots. She didn't like games, and this pledge week had been all about games. She knew it was tradition and meant to build unity, but she'd had enough. She didn't know that she'd be able to let these women push her around much longer without telling them where to go. She took a few deep breaths and tried once again to track the direction the van was going. After a few laps around the block, she gave up and forced herself to stay calm.

The van rolled to a stop, and before the back door was opened for them, Tulley could hear excited activity. Piper opened the door but said nothing for what seemed an eternity.

Finally, she said solemnly, "This will be very important. I hope you're all ready."

Tulley swallowed hard. She didn't want to hear it.

Piper continued, "You are to keep your blindfolds on. One by one, we'll take you out of the van." As if reading Tulley's panicked mind, she added, "We won't let anyone fall, trust us. By now, you should know about trust. We'll get you in a line and then continue."

Two strong hands on either side of the van's doors assisted Tulley out. As she exited, someone else took her over to stand her in the line.

Tulley stood in her place and felt her stomach growl at the strong smell of barbecue on the breeze. It was long past lunchtime, and she wondered if this was just another method of torture the actives thought up.

When the last pledge was out of the van, Piper spoke again. "Your big sisters are standing behind you. They will now remove your blindfolds."

Margeaux, Tulley's big sister, untied the knot in her blindfold and pulled it away. Tulley stood dumbfounded as she took in the scene before her. They were in the same park they had just rested in on their hike. The actives were all there, jumping up and down and yelling and hugging pledges and one another. A giant banner in mulberry and sterling hung between two posts welcoming the newest members of Gamma Alpha Epsilon.

It took a few seconds for it to sink in. Tulley felt Margeaux's arms around her and heard her saying, "Congratulations, Tulley."

She turned to her. "It's over? It's finally over?"

Margeaux flashed a big smile. "Yes, it's over. Now go get some food and beer."

Tulley helped herself to the keg, but the beer didn't taste right. She stood watching everyone celebrate and tried to make herself feel something…some sort of relief or happiness or excitement. All she felt was out of place. Why had she ever thought that would change? She was embarking on a new chapter of her life, and she was filled with more dread than anticipation.

CHAPTER THREE

Soft chanting of solemn hymns emanating from the living room signaled the beginning of the traditional initiation ceremony, officially bringing the recent pledges into the fold and making them active members of the sorority. Sue listened from her room, remembering her own initiation night. She recalled standing outside that very living room with her pledge sisters, each covered only with a white sheet wrapped tightly around her. She had glanced down the line and seen Tabitha framed in her sheet, her full breasts accentuated by it. She hadn't paid much attention to anything else that night.

She cursed herself yet again for falling so hard for Tabitha. She let Tabitha become her world and would have done anything for her. Her grades suffered due to all the energy she focused on her. She had believed she and Tabitha would be together forever.

And so it had come as a total shock their junior year, when Tabitha had told her she wasn't really a lesbian. She told Sue that she'd had fun playing with her, but that she'd met a nice young man and was ready to settle down in real life.

"Real life." Sue could still feel the pain and betrayal all these years later. She had vowed then and there never to let anyone close enough to hurt her again. So far, she'd been very successful in that regard and enjoyed the life she'd made for herself.

Forcing herself back to the present, Sue slid into a pair of tight jeans and a loose green blouse. She didn't want to be in the house during initiation. She was going to leave and let the younger women enjoy this special night. She slipped out the back door and crossed unnoticed to her car.

Sue swore her car knew the route by heart as she maneuvered the streets of Fenton, through the quaint downtown, past all the darkened shops. At eight o'clock on a Sunday evening, they had long since closed. She drove just south of downtown to an area occupied by old garages, boarded-up buildings, and the occasional bar. She pulled into the back parking lot of a nondescript brick building labeled the Top Cat. She walked around to the front door that claimed the business provided grooming for all kinds of cats. The irony made Sue smile as she passed through the black curtain that separated the faux shop front from the lesbian bar.

She surveyed the darkened, smoke-filled room as she felt the floor vibrating from the blaring jukebox. There was a good crowd there for a Sunday, meaning lots of possibilities. She saw one of her regular companions, Jo, shooting pool across the bar. Jo raised up and stared at her. Sue walked to the bar to get a drink before letting Jo see her interest. Her night was improving, though. At least she knew who she'd be going home with.

She ordered a glass of white wine and turned back to the crowd. Jo stood leaning against the wall now, her legs crossed around her cue stick. Her gaze was fixed on Sue. Sue knew the game. No matter how long she waited, Jo would never come to her. If Sue crossed to her, Jo would claim her for the night. She also knew she wanted to prolong the tension for a little while. Sue raised her glass to her lips, peering at Jo over the top of it. Jo showed no change of expression. Someone tapped her with their cue stick and pointed to the table, but still Jo didn't move.

Sue tried to recall how long it had been since she'd enjoyed the pleasures of Jo's tongue. It had been at least two months, and her clit twitched at the memory. Jo was shy, insecure even, but she more than made up for her lack of social skills with her skills at tongue fucking. Sue let out a heavy sigh, resigning herself to crossing the room and admitting to Jo that she wanted her. Although she couldn't imagine Jo had any doubt about that.

She stood next to her, looking up into the deep blue eyes that penetrated through the scraggly dark bangs hanging over them. Without a word, Jo sauntered to the pool table to take her shot. Sue leaned against the wall and took another sip of wine. She wanted Jo to miss her shot so she wouldn't be standing among this group of intimidating butch women all alone.

After three consecutive shots, Jo missed and walked back to tower over Sue. Sue tried to press further into the wall, but the brick had no give. She looked up at Jo, standing only inches from her. She wore a black muscle shirt, exposing tan, muscular arms. Sue wanted to stroke them but felt the familiar awkwardness that accompanied her usual rendezvous with the introverted Jo. She forced herself to look up at Jo's thin, chiseled face with the strong jaw and lips Sue knew could suck like no one else's.

Jo leaned over and rested her forehead on Sue's. "It's been a while. You look good," she said in that low timbre that sent shivers down Sue's back. She felt weak in the knees.

"You look good, too," she managed.

"I'm glad you came over," Jo whispered in her ear before kissing her cheek.

"Me too." Sue leaned her head back as Jo continued kissing and nibbling down her neck. Jo's hand slipped behind her head and tangled in her hair as her mouth closed on Sue's. Sue allowed her eyes to flutter shut as the strong fingers gripped her head and Jo's lips pressed into her. The kiss deepened as Sue ran her tongue along Jo's lips. Jo's lips opened as her tongue wrapped around Sue's and entered her mouth.

"Your shot, Novak," Sue heard just before Jo ended the kiss.

She held on to her shoulders, trying not to let her pull away.

"It's my shot," Jo murmured against her lips.

"But…"

"I'll be back." She plunged her tongue back into Sue's mouth briefly before turning back to the pool table.

Sue admired Jo's long, lithe form as she bent over to take a shot. Her jeans clung to her tight ass, and Sue fought the urge to press against it and cup those firm cheeks. She felt her pussy throb, and when Jo turned back to her, she imagined all sorts of things Jo could do with that cue stick.

Jo seemed to be on the same wavelength as she turned the stick around and ran the thick part up Sue's inner thigh—softly teasing her with just enough pressure to leave her yearning for more.

She smiled wickedly as Sue moved the stick away.

As Jo pressed into her again, Sue said, "I can think of other things I'd rather have running up my thigh."

"Is that right?" Jo nibbled her neck.

"You know it."

Jo claimed her mouth again, her tongue delving deep. Her hands dropped to cup Sue's ass, pulling her close, grinding into her. Sue felt the electricity surge through her body and converge on the nerve center between her legs.

When they broke the kiss, they held each other, breathless.

"Hey! Are you still playing or what?" someone called to Jo.

Sue leaned back and looked at her watch. Jo did the same. It was nine o'clock.

"What time do you have to be home?" Jo asked.

"Midnight."

"Then we don't have time to hang around here," she whispered.

"Or what," Jo called back to her pool buddy and slid an arm around Sue's waist as she guided her out the back door to her waiting truck. "Since we don't have a lot of time, we'll just go to the shop."

Sue liked that idea. She had only been to Jo's house a handful of times. There was something too intimate about that. She much preferred a detached romp in the back room of the auto body shop where Jo worked.

They drove the ten blocks and parked next to the door at the rear of the shop. Before unlocking it, Jo sandwiched Sue against the wall and kissed her again. Sue felt the calloused hands grasping her jaw, holding her in place while their tongues danced yet again.

Jo took her hand when she unlocked the door and led her into the room Jo kept for those occasions when she'd had too many brews at the Top Cat. The scents of the auto body shop greeted Sue as she entered, adding to her arousal. The smells of paint mingled with those she couldn't name, but always associated with Jo, drew her memory back to many pleasurable hours spent there. Her panties were drenched and getting wetter by the minute.

Sue allowed herself to be led to the twin bed along the wall. Jo gently laid her back and slid onto the bed next to her. She ran her hand over Sue, admiration in her eyes.

"You're so fucking hot," Jo said.

Sue's stomach flipped. The desire in Jo's eyes, the feel of her hand skimming her clothed body, the nearness of her thin, taut body, combined to leave Sue almost paralyzed with need.

Slowly but deliberately, Jo unbuttoned Sue's shirt, kissing the bare skin that was left exposed as she went. When Sue lay completely bare, Jo braced herself over her and bent her head to take a hard nipple in her mouth. She sucked the length of it, engulfing the tip of her breast and rolling the hardened nub with her tongue.

Sue grabbed her head, holding her in place as she moaned her pleasure. Her nipple had a direct connection to her clit, which was throbbing in the pool between her legs.

"God, Jo. I love your tongue."

Jo eased her sucking and took the nipple between her teeth, gently tugging on it while her tongue teased just the tip.

"You're making me crazy."

Not letting up on Sue's right nipple, Jo closed her hand over her left, kneading and squeezing. She lazily dragged her fingertips from the base to her nipple from every angle before finally tracing the nipple itself, causing it to grow tighter before pinching and twisting it.

Sue grasped the sheet under her. Her hips moved with a mind of their own, gyrating against Jo. She grabbed Jo's hand and pressed it into the crotch of her jeans so she could feel the wetness seeping through.

Jo pulled her hand away and went to work on the button and zipper while she moved her mouth to the other breast. She slipped her hand inside Sue's jeans and drew her hand back and forth above the bikini panties.

Sue's skin rippled at Jo's touch. Every inch of her was covered with goose bumps as she craved for that hand to slide beneath the panties. Jo kissed up Sue's neck to her ear as her hand moved down between her legs and pressed the sopping panties into her hot cunt.

"Holy fuck, you're wet," Jo murmured into her ear before licking inside it.

She pulled her panties to the side and slipped two fingers inside. Sue arched her hips, relishing the feeling but needing more.

"Fuck me, Jo. I need you to fuck me."

Jo moved away, and together they managed to get Sue's jeans and panties off. Sue spread her legs as wide as she could while Jo took her place between them. Jo dragged her tongue slowly up one inner thigh, then stopped millimeters from Sue's rigid clit. She did the same up the other inner thigh and stopped again, this time poised over the pulsating nerve center.

"Please," Sue whimpered. She could feel Jo's breath and needed her mouth on her.

Jo extended her long tongue and licked deep inside Sue's slick, hot pussy, then between her swollen lips and up to circle her clit.

Sue was getting dizzy. She had never been this aroused without release. She didn't know how much longer she would last. Every muscle in her body was poised for what she was sure to come, she just didn't know when.

"Please don't tease me. Please."

Jo buried her tongue inside her and covered every inch. With short, quick movements, she licked the tenderness at the tip of her tongue. With long, determined strokes, she licked the length of the walls, stopping to press her tongue into Sue's most sensitive spot.

She replaced her tongue with three fingers and moved them in and out at a frantic pace while she sucked Sue's clit between her teeth and licked the base of it with rhythmic determination.

Sue bucked and writhed against her, taking her fingers deeper and making her suck harder. Suddenly, everything went black. There was no sight or sound, only the feelings Jo was creating between her legs. She felt the volcano in her soul erupt, shooting white-hot lava all over her body, to every extremity, and she plummeted into the abyss of a powerful orgasm. She floated out there, looking at her body spread-eagle on the bed, sailing on the feelings for what seemed like forever before slowly returning to Earth. She had yet to catch her breath when she was catapulted into the atmosphere again as Jo continued her ministrations.

When she finally settled down, Jo carefully pulled her fingers from the suction of her pussy and kissed her way up to her mouth, sharing the deliciousness of her orgasm with her.

"My God, you're wonderful," Jo whispered, pulling Sue close.

"You're not so bad yourself." Sue rolled over and rested her head on Jo's chest. "Mmm, you feel good."

"I'm not even doing anything." Jo laughed.

"I love the way your laugh sounds in your chest," she said dreamily, listening to the deep murmur.

"Is that right?" Jo stroked Sue's hair, and Sue felt her eyes drifting shut.

"Hey, Sleeping Beauty," Sue heard through the fog.

"Come on. Time to wake up."

"What?" Sue asked, stretching.

"You fell asleep, beautiful. But it's time for you to get up."

"Why's that?" Sue asked, still unable to open her eyes.

"It's eleven thirty."

"No!"

"I'm afraid so. Get up and get dressed and we'll go get your car."

As Sue got out of bed, she asked, "Did you get some sleep, too?"

Jo laughed. "I'm not much of the cuddle and sleep type."

"So where were you while I slept?"

"I was putting some Bondo on a sixty-nine Charger."

"Sorry I was such an exciting date."

"You were wonderful. As usual."

When Sue let herself into her car, she was wide-awake. She was also congratulating herself on her decision to hit the Top Cat that night. Jo Novak had been just what the doctor ordered.

❖

With the initiation complete, it was time to take the new members out to celebrate. The girls put on their jeans and the new jerseys with Greek letters on them. Car keys were confiscated, and big sisters assumed full responsibility for their charges.

"Are you ready to party?" Margeaux asked Tulley.

"Are we really going to a bar?" Tulley asked as they walked to Margeaux's car. "I mean, it's not like I haven't snuck into bars before, but are you going to tell me that a whole group of us are going to walk in and no one is going to card us?"

"It's all good. We're going to The Asylum. It's a beer joint owned by an old BI guy."

"Oh, that's cool. So that's where all the Beta Iotas hang out, huh?"

Margeaux smiled and nudged her. "Why? Do you have your eye on a certain BI guy?"

Tulley blushed, much to her chagrin. "No. It's just that, since their house is across the street from ours, it might be good to know a little bit about them."

Margeaux looked unimpressed. "Okay. But yes. They hang out there. There are a few frats that do and a few sororities. Not the real snooty ones or anything. Because you're not going to find an appletini at The Asylum."

Tulley laughed. "Very cool. Because I'm much more into beer than foofy drinks."

"Yeah. I kinda got that about you."

Not sure what she meant, Tulley decided to let the comment go and tried to relax. She started thinking about other GAEs and decided there were a few, Danielle for example, she couldn't imagine at a beer bar.

"So all GAEs hang out there?"

"Well, not all. Like any other group of people, we all have different tastes."

"Will the other types be there tonight?"

"At least in the beginning. It's tradition. Why?"

"No reason. I was just wondering." Tulley felt much better knowing she might not have to spend the evening partying with the likes of Danielle and her group.

The Asylum was rocking when Tulley and Margeaux walked in. The jukebox was playing a Green Day song, and most of the long wooden tables were occupied with groups of college kids talking, laughing, or playing drinking games.

The bar ran along the far wall and was made of the same dark wood as the rest of the tables. They walked up, and Margeaux asked for two glasses. She handed one to Tulley.

"It looks like our tables are over in the corner." She led the way to two long tables filled with women Tulley recognized and a lot of guys she didn't. Margeaux showed no hesitation as she sidled in between the kids on the crowded bench and made room for herself and Tulley. She reached for the pitcher and filled their glasses.

"Welcome." She touched her glass to Tulley's.

"Thanks." Tulley took a drink, and the table burst into chorus.

"Drink! Drink! Drink! Drink!"

Margeaux whispered in Tulley's ear. "That means they want you to chug the whole glass."

Tulley drained her glass, and as soon as she put it back on the table, someone filled it again. Suddenly, sorority life didn't seem so bad. She had a bar where she could get served. There were lots of fun-loving people around looking for a good time. And so far, the beer was free.

The group started cheering again as one of Tulley's pledge sisters downed her beer in two swallows. The raucous crowd screamed at her chugging talent. Tulley clapped and yelled, as well. A blond BI guy with blue eyes and a sparkling smile patted her on the back. "I think it's your turn again."

Happy to oblige, she opened her mouth and finished her beer as quickly as her sister. The evening went on, with more chugging and more laughing and yelling. The clean-cut blond took her hand later and led her to the jukebox.

"Help me choose some music," he yelled in her ear.

She could barely stand and was grateful for his strong arm around her. They both almost fell over once, they were laughing so hard at his imitation of Beyoncé. Tulley helped him pick out music and stumbled with him back to the table.

Margeaux looked up at her as she tried to sit. "I think you've had enough," she said as Tulley practically fell into her lap and burst into laughter.

"But I'm having fun."

"Yeah. We're having a good time," the frat boy piped up. "If you need to get going, I'll make sure she gets home."

"Yes," Margeaux said. "But to whose home?"

She stood and pulled Tulley with her. Tulley watched as Margeaux caught the gazes of a few other big sisters and pointed to the clock. Tulley glanced up and saw that it was close to midnight and she guessed some of the others probably had early classes. She stumbled as Margeaux half guided, half dragged her to the car. She allowed herself to be poured into the passenger seat and tried to remain conscious as Margeaux slid behind the wheel.

Margeaux laughed the whole way back to the house as Tulley went on and on about how much fun she'd had.

"You may be drunk, but I have to say, this is the first time I've ever seen you really relax."

Margeaux pulled into the driveway of the sorority house.

"Why are we here?" Tulley slurred.

"I don't want to drop you off and worry about you getting to your dorm room. I'll feel better knowing you're safe and sound here." She helped her into the house and sat her down on a couch in the large den. "I'm going to get some blankets for you. Go ahead and get comfortable. You'll be sleeping on this couch."

Tulley stripped to her boxers and bra and passed out, not even waking up when Margeaux returned to cover her with the blankets.

❖

Sue changed into her sweats and checked the clock. It was midnight. Time to make sure everyone in the house was in bed. Or at least in their rooms. She checked every room on the main floor and was happy to find that, after such a big night, everyone had managed to get to bed on time. As she approached the den, she heard soft noises. She paused and smiled as she saw four young women she didn't know, one on each couch. She had seen that before. After all, it had been initiation night, which meant a big party at The Asylum.

As she turned to leave, the brunette on one couch along the far wall caught her eye. She walked over and looked down at the baby butch snoring softly. She resisted the urge to brush her bangs off her forehead. There was an innocence about this one that drew Sue to her. Suddenly, the satisfaction Jo gave her was wearing off, replaced by a new twitch as she stared at the thin lips, parted slightly as the girl slept.

She sighed heavily as she turned to leave the room. As she slid into bed, she questioned again if, at twenty-four, it was time to give up the job as RA. That girl on the couch couldn't have been more than eighteen or nineteen, yet she was the reason for the smile on Sue's face as she drifted off to sleep.

CHAPTER FOUR

Thursday evening finally rolled around. It was a time Tulley had dreaded since Sunday. Now that she was initiated, Tulley knew Thursdays would mean getting together with different fraternities and partying with them at socials. After her fun at The Asylum, Tulley was looking forward to those. But not this particular Thursday. This evening was the ceremony known as flower pinning.

It was tradition on the Thursday after initiation that the new members of the sorority and fraternity get introduced to and welcomed by the older members in a semi-formal ceremony followed by a festive consumption of beer and champagne. The new members would be introduced as couples to the group. The new fraternity brother would pin a rosebud on the new sorority sister. They'd kiss and walk off the stage so the next couple could be introduced.

As a rule, flower pinnings were less rowdy than regular Thursday socials. Tulley wasn't much in the mood for partying anyway as she sat on the narrow bed in her dorm room and pulled on her second pair of nylons. When they ran too, she threw them across the room. Or attempted to—nylons didn't travel far when thrown.

"Fuck!" She crossed to her three-drawer dresser to get another pair.

"I still don't understand why you're doing this," her social activist roommate, Sienna, said. "It's just an augmentation of the struggle of the poor against the wealthy, and you're taking the stand that you're of the 'haves' and don't give a shit about the 'have nots.'"

Tulley turned and just stared at her.

Sienna took another hit off her joint and handed it Tulley's way.

"No thanks. I need to get ready and get out of here." She stood, nylons finally on, and slipped her black silk empire-waist dress over her head and smoothed it down her thighs. She slid her feet into low pumps and looked at herself in the full-length mirror.

"I don't know why you let them make you do this. That so isn't the Tulley I know standing there."

"You're not helping."

"I'm just saying."

"So I look like a clown." She grimaced at the reflection of her face, covered in makeup. It was true that the mascara that framed her eyes called attention to them, but she felt like a fool. She turned to Sienna. "And so I hate dresses."

"Yeah. Outside of that."

"I'm out of here."

"Should I wait up?"

"Very funny."

"That's right. You might find some handsome Richie Rich out there you can marry and join the country club with and dress like this all the time for and…"

Tulley quickly closed the door behind her so she didn't have to listen to her stoned roommate's ramblings anymore. She took the elevator to the first floor, where she ran into her pledge sister Kelly, who was wearing a short sleeved, green satin, form-fitting dress with pearl earrings and necklace. Tulley wondered how Kelly could look so normal in jeans and a sweatshirt and yet pull off the semi-formal look so naturally.

"You look great, Tulley. Wow, that's some dress."

"Thanks. You look nice, too." Tulley's stomach churned. Compliments had never been easy for her to give or receive. "Are you walking to the house, too?"

"Walking? No way. My big sis is giving me a ride. Do you want to join us?"

"That would be great. I can't imagine walking across campus in these." She pointed to her shoes.

Kelly laced her arm through Tulley's and together they exited the air-conditioned dormitory and braced themselves against the Northern California April heat. Even at five thirty in the evening, the temperatures still hovered near ninety-five degrees.

They walked down the steps and out to the street where Kelly's big sister, Lorraine, was waiting.

"Are you two excited?" she asked as she pulled out and maneuvered through milling students to get to the main road.

"I am," Kelly said. "I wonder who my date will be. Have you seen their new members, Tulley? There are some hotties."

"They're not technically our dates, are they?" Tulley hoped she didn't sound as panicked as she felt. "I mean, we just get introduced with them, right? We're not expected to hang out with them all night, are we?"

Lorraine looked at her in the rearview mirror and laughed. "Relax. You're not required to do anything after the ceremony except have fun."

Tulley eased back in her seat and tried to relax, but she wasn't sure how she could have fun dressed in her ridiculous getup. Even if she'd wanted to dance, which she was sure she wouldn't, the shoes she was wearing would make that impossible. She tried to think of the positive side as they pulled up to the house, but she couldn't find one.

The house was abuzz when they walked in. Everyone was all dressed up, and every available mirror had four or five sisters in front of it, jostling to check their makeup. Tulley looked for a friendly face in the crowd and spotted Livie hugging a wall in the trophy room, just off the entryway. The trophy room was where they hung composites, pictures of all the active members, going back ten years, as well as trophies from sorority softball tournaments and other competitions the sisters participated in.

"You look nervous," she said.

"I am," Livie said. "What about you?"

"Terrified."

"You look pretty."

"Thanks." Tulley stared at the navy blue dress with the sailor collar that Livie was wearing and forced herself to say, "You look nice, too."

Just then, Danielle walked up with her group. She stopped and stood in front of Tulley wearing a champagne-colored halter dress, which showcased her long blond hair and bright green eyes. She examined Tulley. "There's a mirror available in the front room. You might want to touch up your makeup."

They walked off with their noses in the air.

"Maybe we should," Livie said.

"Why? I mean, you can, but I'm not going to. I think I have enough of this stuff on already."

Livie had yet to move when Piper appeared in the doorway.

"Ladies!" she called. "Ladies, please. I need all new initiates to join me in the entry hall."

They gathered in the large marbled foyer, thankful not to have to form a line for once.

"It's time to go across the street and join the BI guys. A reminder of how this will go. You will be paired up with one of their new initiates. You will wait on the side of the stage until the emcee nods to you. You cross to the center of the stage. Their new initiate will pin a rose on you, kiss you, then the two of you turn and walk off the stage.

"Now this is your first official social and I want to remind you that we want you to have fun and meet new people. We also want you to keep in mind that tonight, like any other time, you are representing Gamma Alpha Epsilon sorority. Please conduct yourselves accordingly."

Tulley heard Danielle and her friends giggling behind her and expected Piper to comment on it. Instead, Piper just smiled. Tulley rolled her eyes and took a deep breath. She just had to get through the introductions. Then she could lose herself in the crowd of sixty other GAEs who would be there.

"Honey, relax," Kelly told her as they crossed the street.

"Is it that obvious?"

"Yes. We're all nervous. But you look terrified."

"I don't do so well being the center of attention. On stage, you know. Especially with some strange guy kissing me."

Livie joined them. "Maybe he'll be really cute and a great kisser."

"Yeah," Kelly agreed.

Tulley's stomach roiled. She was beginning to wonder if she could pull this off. Maybe she should have called in sick.

The men of Beta Iota had gathered on their porch, looking dapper in their suits and ties. They began to serenade their guests with a beautiful ballad about their hearts belonging to the women of Gamma Alpha Epsilon.

The sorority sisters clapped when they were through, and the men walked down the stairs and each took the arm of one and escorted her to the backyard. The yard was bordered with tiki torches. A stage was set up at the far end with steps on either side. Two poles stood at either end of it and lights hung between them. It was very different from the way the yard usually looked.

One of the BI guys, a particularly handsome brunette with a bright smile and charismatic personality, took the microphone on stage.

"Welcome, ladies of Gamma Alpha Epsilon. My name's Steve and I'll be the emcee for the evening. As we all know, tonight is the time to show off our newly initiated members. I know we Beta Iotas have a very handsome new crop and I've gotta say, I'm seeing some very fine-looking new ladies in your group." He winked at Danielle.

"So let's get the newbies to gather over here to my left and we'll get the ceremony started. While everyone's taking their place, please help yourself to some champagne or beer from the bar in the back corner."

Tulley moved to the side of the stage with the rest of the new initiates. A lanky redhead walked over to her.

"Hi. I'm Todd. May I escort you?"

She looked up and saw dark green eyes that seemed innocent enough.

"I'm Tulley. Sure."

"It's nice to meet you, Tulley."

They took their place, seventh in line. There were more young women than men, so the men who went first would come back and escort the other GAEs. Tulley watched as Steve nodded to the first couple. They walked up, her arm linked through his. When they reached the middle of the stage, he took a rosebud out of a basket that sat on a barstool and carefully, although somewhat awkwardly, pinned it to her dress. They faced the crowd as Steve introduced them. Then they kissed briefly and chastely before turning to walk off the other end of the stage.

When the second couple got on stage, the same routine was performed. The third couple, Danielle and a handsome, clean-cut guy, were greeted with cheers as they crossed to the middle of the stage. He looked out to the crowd and flashed a winning smile that went well with his arrogant stride. He raised his arm and twirled his fist in the air. The BI guys yelled louder.

It probably would have been awkward for most guys to pin a rosebud on the halter of Danielle's dress, but her escort had no problem. He slid his hand between the material and her skin as casually as if they'd been together for years.

Steve introduced the couple, and with no preamble, her escort kissed her hard, his tongue obviously deep in her mouth. Her body stiffened visibly at first and then she appeared to relax and go with it. When the kiss finally ended, he looked back to the crowd, which had worked into a frenzy watching the kiss.

Tulley couldn't believe what she'd just seen. What made it worse was Todd cheering and clapping as loud as anyone. Her stomach knotted tighter with each introduction. Finally, it was their turn.

She linked her arm through his as they walked onto the stage. Her knees went weak when she heard the group chanting, "Todd! Todd! Todd! Todd!"

Todd looked out at the crowd and smiled. Tulley added that to the unease she was feeling as she wondered if her dress was hanging right and if her hair was still spiked just right or if it had fallen.

After Todd had pinned the rosebud to her and Steve announced them, Todd placed his open mouth on hers and forced his tongue inside. His lips felt like engorged worms, fat and slimy, and his tongue triggered her gag reflex. She struggled against it and tried to pull away, only to feel his grip tighten. His tongue continued to make laps inside her mouth, running along her gums and her cheeks. She fought to keep her tongue out of its way.

When Todd finally stood and Tulley was able to breathe again, she tried to exit the stage as quickly as possible. She almost pulled away from Todd, who was strutting slowly, accepting accolades from his brothers. By the time they got to the stairs on the other side, Tulley could feel the tears welling. She admonished herself not to let them spill over. At the base of the stairs, Todd turned to her, but before he could say anything, she slipped away and made a beeline to the bar. Relieved to be surrounded by her sisters, she quickly chugged one beer and then another. She was starting to calm down when Danielle walked up and asked for a glass of champagne.

"Well, that was embarrassing," she said to Tulley before taking a sip.

Tulley stood dumbfounded. She'd never imagined Danielle would see her side of any situation.

"I mean the way you acted up there. Like you've never had a guy kiss you before."

"He wasn't supposed to kiss me like that. Not all of us like strangers sticking their tongues down our throats."

"It's all in fun," Danielle said condescendingly. "You didn't have to act so disgusted."

Tulley couldn't believe her ears. "I didn't appreciate it. I don't open my mouth and let any man slobber all over me like some people."

She became aware that the group of their sisters had closed in around them. Nobody was saying anything, but she felt like she was back on the stage, her every movement being scrutinized.

"Well, maybe you should consider it. He might have been the best you'll ever have."

"What's that supposed to mean?"

Danielle looked down at her. "I mean, I hope you're not holding out for something better. It's not like you're such a great catch."

Tulley refused to be goaded. She shook her head and turned away.

"Or maybe there's another reason you didn't like the kiss."

"And what might that be?"

"Just look at you. I bet you're gay." She sneered.

Tulley spun around and got in Danielle's face. "What in the hell did you just say?"

Piper, Margeaux, Livie, Kelly, as well as several other members, quickly stepped between them.

"Calm down. Both of you. Your behavior is unbecoming of a Gamma Alpha Epsilon," Piper said.

"Her behavior on stage was," Danielle said.

"No," a woman Tulley recognized as Sue, the RA of the house, joined in. She was slightly older than they were, in her mid-twenties with long blond hair. Tulley hadn't had the chance to get to know Sue, but she appreciated her backing. Something about her calmed Tulley. And there was something else she couldn't quite name. The woman's green eyes flashed in anger. "She had every right to feel violated up there. What's not acceptable is not that you called her a lesbian, but you said it like an insult. GAEs don't tolerate homophobia."

"I can't imagine that we tolerate lap lickers, either," Danielle threw over her shoulder as she pushed through the crowd and sidled up with a group of BI guys.

"I'd love to kill that fucking bitch." Tulley stared after Danielle.

Margeaux wrapped an arm around her and squeezed. "She's not worth it. Have another beer."

"No, thanks. Seems to me it's about time for me to head home."

Lorraine stepped in. "Why don't we go to The Asylum, have a few beers, and forget this place?"

"That sounds good. I'd like to get out of here, too," Livie said.

On the drive over, Tulley started to question whether she had overreacted. But she knew she hadn't. She had been raised to believe she didn't have to let anybody do anything to her body that she didn't want. And that included a disgustingly sloppy kiss.

She was happy to be forming this tight circle of friends in the sorority. She was certain they would help make membership less painful at least.

❖

The lights were off in Sue's room. Candlelight danced off every surface. She had wanted to play low music, but she wanted to be able to hear if anyone came in even more. She could still hear the party raging across the street. She felt reasonably safe she would be uninterrupted.

Sue slid out of her clothes and into a short green satin robe, then lay on her bed and closed her eyes, visualizing those blue eyes as she moved her hand under the robe and stroked her breast. She teased her nipple until it was so taut it ached. As she slipped her hand down her belly, she pictured those eyes and all the emotions that had flashed in them.

She felt for the awkward baby butch, whom she now knew as Tulley, so uncomfortable in that dress and so humiliated when that geek forced himself on her. She was aroused by the anger that flashed when she defended herself against that blond bitch.

She slid her hand between her legs, past her engorged clit, and into her hot pussy, already slick with need. Refusing to focus on the fact that what made Tulley angry was being called a lesbian, Sue let herself imagine those same eyes dark with passion as she lay over her, that young, firm body pressed into hers just before she dipped her mouth to kiss her fiercely.

It was Tulley's fingers inside her then, driving deeper, faster, in and out, while Sue panted harder, craving release. The butch was rough, but not overly so, as she pummeled Sue's pussy, almost daring her not to climax. She threw her head back as the strong fingers pressed into her clit and threw her over the edge with such force her whole body tensed.

When at last the spasms had ceased, Sue reluctantly withdrew her fingers and sucked them clean. She wanted to drift to sleep but had to stay up to make sure everyone was home safe and sound. She smiled as she walked to the kitchen to get some juice, thinking how nice it would be if the baby butch ended up sleeping on the couch again. She'd behave, of course. But it was sure fun to fantasize about.

CHAPTER FIVE

On the last night of summer break, the night before the new members moved into the house, Sue's mind was blank, her world void, save for the sensations on her nipples and between her legs. Nema, her bedmate for the night, was a mistress at delivering just the right amount of pain to deliver paramount pleasure. They had been at it all night. It was one of the few nights she didn't need to be home by midnight or two o'clock. The house was empty. The few stragglers from last year had finally moved out, and the new residents wouldn't move in until the next day. Sue and Nema had met up at a Harley exhibit where Nema was showing her Softail Cross Bones.

"Nice ride," Sue had whispered from behind when she found her at the display.

"I'm glad you remember," Nema said, turning to give her a tight hug. "I'm glad you showed up."

"It was good to hear from you. Thanks for calling."

"Well, you don't want to spend your afternoon hanging out here, so why don't we go somewhere and grab a beer or something?"

"Sounds good. Are we taking your bike?"

"Nah. I have to leave it here. You'll have to drive."

"Not a problem. As long as you promise to drive later." She cocked an eyebrow at her.

"Whatever the lady wants."

They crossed the parking lot to Sue's car, walking so close their shoulders rubbed. Nema's proximity had Sue aroused to the point she would have gladly driven straight to her house. She could feel her nipples hardening and knew they were forming tents under her white spaghetti-strapped tank top. She swallowed hard as moisture pooled in her panties and slowly began trickling down her thigh. Sue hoped against hope the trickle stopped before it got past her short shorts.

"So how you been?" Nema asked as she slid into the passenger seat.

"Not bad."

"You look good. Damned good."

"So do you." Sue gazed into the dark brown eyes staring at her and felt her pussy clench at the need she saw there.

Nema turned to face forward and strapped in. "How about we head out to the river for a few pitchers?"

Sue sighed heavily and tried to stop her hands from shaking before turning the key in the ignition.

"You gonna be okay?" Nema asked.

Sue blushed. "Sure, why?"

Nema stretched an arm out behind her. "You seem a little quivery."

"That could be the understatement of the year."

Nema laughed, a deep, resonant sound that sent hot chills coursing through Sue's body. Nema ran her fingers along Sue's neck and slowly slid them under the dangling silver and malachite earrings she wore.

"These are nice."

Sue swallowed hard and gripped the steering wheel tighter. "Thank you." She breathed a sigh of relief when Nema faced forward and seemed to settle in for the drive.

The four-mile drive to the river was torture for Sue. It started with Nema's hand resting lightly on her thigh. After the first mile, her hand was lazily stroking the length of it.

"Are you sure you want to go grab a beer?" Sue glanced quickly at Nema's hand. "We can always go straight to your place."

"Aw, come on." Nema nibbled on her neck and slid her hand just under the leg of her shorts. "Why do that when there's so much teasing still to be done? Turn down this road." She pointed to a dirt road.

"I think it's the next one."

"Humor me."

"Fine." Sue turned left and slowed as the dust flew all around them. She held tight to the wheel as the car pitched from right to left, bouncing in and out of potholes on the unpaved ground.

"Pull over here." Nema pointed a tan arm in the direction of a copse of palm trees.

Sue drove into the middle of them and stopped. "Where are we?"

"In the middle of nowhere."

She rolled her eyes and then looked around. "It looks that way. I don't see a house or building anywhere near here."

"There are some up by the orchards." Nema took off her seat belt and leaned into Sue. She kissed her neck, feathery soft kisses that made Sue moan. She playfully flicked her earlobe with her tongue before sucking it in her mouth, twirling it on her tongue.

Sue's eyes were closed as she clumsily reached for Nema. She felt her head and pulled her to her, her mouth automatically closing on Nema's. Her heart raced as she tasted those familiar lips and felt her strong, soft tongue gliding into her mouth.

Nema reached over and unhooked Sue's seat belt, then lowered her seat before reclining her own.

"What are you doing?"

"Getting comfortable." She clumsily placed a leg over the console and kissed Sue again while sliding her hand under the flimsy tank top. "I forgot how long your nipples get."

Sue barely heard her. She could only feel. She felt Nema's skilled hands twisting and pulling, kneading and caressing. She felt her teeth and lips on her neck. She tangled her fingers through Nema's long black hair as she moaned in pleasure. When she felt Nema's hand slide down to play with the waistband of her shorts, she spread her legs as wide as she could.

She gasped as she felt fingers slide past her hard clit and tease her swollen lips. When Nema entered her, she arched her hips to urge her deeper, faster. Nema kissed her passionately, her tongue claiming her mouth the way her fingers claimed her cunt. Sue was dizzy as she neared her climax only to feel Nema stop.

She barely found her voice. "Huh?"

Nema looked over the top of her head. "We may have company."

"What?" Sue tried to spin to look.

"Just stay put. Maybe they'll keep driving."

It seemed like forever before Sue heard tires on the dirt just behind them.

"Shit," Nema spat, getting out of the car. "You'd better sit up."

Sue readjusted her seat and craned her neck to watch the scene unfolding.

Nema stood as two very large men got out of a half-ton Chevy pickup.

The larger one said, "Pullins, what are you doing here?"

She motioned to Sue in the car. "My friend was in a bad way. I was just trying to comfort her. We were on the way to The Landing. She started losing it, so I had her pull over."

"You know this is private property." His voice was soft, not intimidating. "If we start letting you hang out here, we'll have to let everyone. We've been through this."

"I know, I know. It was poor judgment on my part. We'll take off and it won't happen again."

She extended her hand to the man, who took it in a firm grip. She smiled, and as she got back in the car, she called out, "You're going to want to wash that hand before you go near your wife."

"I can't believe you said that," Sue said.

Nema laughed. "It's true. I didn't have to warn him, you know."

As Sue started backing out, Nema sucked her fingers. "You do taste good, lover."

"I'd like you to find out from a little closer encounter."

"Oh, I plan to. Now let's go to The Landing. I've worked up quite a thirst."

"As have I. I don't believe there's any liquid in my body above my waist."

"Be sure you keep it that way."

"I don't know that I have any choice as long as you're around." Sue stopped and looked over at Nema. "You're not really going to make me go to The Landing, are you? You've got me a wet mess. I need you, Nema. I need you *now*."

The dark eyes bore into hers for what seemed like an eternity before she finally relented. "Okay. Let's go to my place. We'll finally be able to take our time for once."

The afternoon turned into evening and then night as Nema treated Sue to myriad pleasures and pains.

She fastened nipple clamps on Sue then placed the chain that ran between them in her mouth. As Nema's mouth worked its magic on Sue's cunt and Sue's head thrashed as she closed in on her orgasm, the chain tightened the clamps, sending white heat of painful pleasure to her core.

Sue loved the conflicting responses Nema could elicit and let the white heat blind her and lead her soaring into orgasm after orgasm.

When Sue's climaxes had ceased, Nema clipped a clamp on Sue's still hard clitoris and went to work sucking and biting her erect nipples. Sue grasped her head and held her there, clearly needing everything Nema was giving her.

Nema slid a hand inside Sue's hot pussy, driving deep, then pressing the slick walls as she pulled out. Sue was barely breathing by the time Nema took the clamp off her clit and with one swipe of her thumb sent molten lava flowing through Sue's veins as she came three more times, each orgasm racking her body harder than the one before.

"You sure know how to treat a lady," Sue said.

"You sure know how not to act like one."

"Sue? Sue?" Beth Lyons, one of the oldest actives, sat on Sue's bed holding a steaming cup of coffee. "Sue?" She shook her. "You need to get up. The new house members will start moving in in a couple of hours. You need to get ready."

Sue opened an eye and glared at the clock. She'd only gotten home a few hours earlier, and she wasn't in any shape to function. She pulled her sheet over her head.

Beth laughed and pulled the sheet off. "Come on, Sue."

She rolled onto her back. "Are you sure? Can't I sleep for a few more days?"

"Sit up."

Sue groaned as she made her way to a sitting position and slid her back against the wall as she gratefully accepted the coffee. She took a healthy sip and looked back at the clock again.

"What time are they supposed to start getting here?"

"Nine o'clock."

"Ugh."

"Yeah. I strongly suggest you finish that and then hit the shower. You've got to look decent today. If not for the members, then for their parents who'll be helping them move in."

"I'm getting too old for this."

"Age is just a number."

"Nice try. I feel very old right now."

"Well, maybe if you came home before five a.m.," Beth playfully chastised her.

"It's my only night of the year to go out and play," Sue said.

"Why don't you ever tell anyone where you go when you play?"

"Because I'm old and the places I go would be boring for you kids."

"You never know." Beth stood. "Now get ready."

Sue sat there finishing her coffee and wondered if paranoia accompanied old age. No one had ever even hinted at an interest in where she went or what she did on her time away from the house. She shook it off and chalked it up to looking like crap, then gingerly walked down the hall to the shower, glad there was no one around to question how sore she was. She smiled at the memories but knew she needed to snap out of it and get ready for the day.

Refreshed from her shower, Sue traded coffee for an old-fashioned bottle of Pepsi and took her place on the whitewashed porch swing to watch the parade of new initiates moving into the house. There were plenty of actives milling about for general help, but she needed to be there in case anything extraordinary came up. Also, it wasn't uncommon for the older members to want to introduce their little sisters to her rather than waiting until the official introduction.

She sat in her khaki shorts and pink T-shirt and watched as the new crop of young women struggled with their possessions. There were four wide steps to climb to reach the porch that ran the length of the house. The girls had to maneuver their belongings through the single front door and up the staircase. Sue had learned it was best to stay out of the way but remain visible. Her perch on the swing made that possible.

❖

Tulley directed her brother Nathan through the quiet streets of midday Fenton until he pulled his Chevy Silverado pickup truck in front of the sorority house where she would live for the next year. Her stomach churned as she watched some of her housemates milling about on the lawn and porch. She saw a few of Danielle's friends but didn't see either of her roommates, Livie or Kelly. There were a few other pledge sisters there who seemed to be having a good time.

They got out of the truck and dropped the tailgate, then slid her suitcases and boxes of belongings to the edge of the bed.

"You ready?" Nathan asked.

"It's not like this stuff's that heavy. Come on. Let's just get this over with."

He laughed. "You gonna enjoy it this much all year?"

"I doubt it. Now drop the subject," she said as they got to the bottom of the steps.

They climbed the steps but had to wait, as there were two women ahead of them. One turned while she waited and her gaze immediately met Tulley's. They had all day to move in and Tulley couldn't believe she was waiting her turn behind Danielle.

Danielle didn't try to hide her disdain when she saw her. Tulley tried not to let her disgust show, but she couldn't help laughing when one of Danielle's boxes began to slip from her grasp. Much to her dismay, her own brother put her things down and reached forward to catch Danielle's before they hit the ground.

Nathan gently handed Danielle's things to her then turned back to Tulley.

"What's your hurry?" she heard Danielle say. Tulley's skin crawled. She couldn't possibly be talking to her brother, could she?

"No hurry. Just didn't want to be in the way."

"Oh, how could a nice looking guy like you possibly be in the way?"

Tulley watched Nathan blush and wanted nothing else but to kill both of them. When Danielle slipped her arm around him and pulled him toward her, Tulley thought her head would blow off.

"We've still got to wait until they get theirs up the stairs." Danielle motioned to the duo in front of her. "So why don't we get to know each other a little better while we wait?"

"If you're sure you don't mind."

"Not at all."

Tulley couldn't believe this was happening. Her own brother was betraying her for Danielle. While they were ogling each other, she took the opportunity to check Danielle out unnoticed. Her shorts left little to the imagination as they showed more of her ass than they covered. Her golden hair was pulled back in a loose ponytail, and her makeup was perfect.

Tulley looked down at her own outfit—cargo shorts and her maroon shirt with the sorority letters on the front. She had a baseball cap on to control her hair and, as usual, she wore no makeup. She was there to move in, not win a beauty pageant. Her musings were interrupted when she felt someone watching her.

Looking around, she saw no one paying attention to her until her gaze lighted on Sue, the RA, sitting on the porch swing. Tulley immediately flashed back to the flower pinning and Sue's intervention and support that night. She found it odd that Sue continued to stare at her, even after she'd been caught. It didn't bother her as much as she thought it would.

Tulley realized she hadn't thanked Sue for her actions the previous spring, and somehow the thought of walking over to her at the moment terrified and excited her. Movement out of the corner of her eye drew her attention away.

Nathan was helping Danielle carry her things in the house and up the stairs. She gathered up some of her stuff, not wanting to wait for him to come back and help her. So far, her day had started lousy and gotten worse. She didn't hold out much hope that it was going to get any better.

Chapter Six

Tulley lay on the bottom bunk, arms folded under her head. Her new roommate Kelly sat with her while Livie, their third, sat on her own bed. They laughed as they exchanged stories of their summer vacations.

"He actually asked you to climb into his backseat? Right in front of your parents' house?" Kelly wiped away tears.

"He *did*. As if," Livie said. "And he was so gross anyway."

"I can't believe you went out with him," Tulley added, her stomach turning. "I mean, if he was that gross."

"I was bored. And my friend promised she'd owe me if I went out with him. She had a date and didn't want to hang out with her cousin."

"What did she end up paying you?" Tulley asked.

Before she could answer, Mindy, another new resident in the house, poked her head in their room. "Everyone is supposed to go down to the front room. I guess we're having a meeting."

"What about?" Livie asked her.

"Don't know. I'm just rounding everyone up." She disappeared down the hall.

Tulley playfully kicked Kelly in the butt so she'd get up and let her out.

"I'm not in the mood for a meeting," Tulley complained.

"Ah, come on," Livie said. "There have to be some rules about living here. I would imagine now would be a good time to learn them."

They walked downstairs together and even managed not to let Danielle's disapproving look ruin their mood. They sat on one couch against the far wall and watched as their sisters paraded downstairs and sat in the folding chairs set up in the center of the room.

Soon the room was abuzz with excited chatter as the new residents greeted each other, seemingly happy to see one another after their summer vacation. Tulley watched the activity, but with each new person who came in, she tried to push herself further into the corner of the couch. She felt nauseated as the reality dawned on her that she would be living with all these women for the next year.

"Can I get you all to settle down, please?" A voice carried across the room. "Come on, now. This doesn't have to take too long, but I need you all to focus this way, okay?"

Slowly, the voices quieted and they all faced Sue, who stood at the front of the room.

"First of all, I want to welcome each and every one of you to the Gamma Alpha Epsilon house—" Her speech was interrupted by rowdy cheers. "I'm glad you're all so excited. I think we're going to have a great year. You all definitely represent two of the best pledge classes we've seen in a while."

There was more clapping and cheering, but Tulley didn't participate. Memories of pledging washed over her and her blood ran cold. She couldn't believe the rest of her class looked back on it favorably.

Sue laughed. "Wow. I hope you're all still this excited to be here after a few weeks."

Tulley watched Sue run her gaze over the group, pausing briefly when it landed on her. She felt the corners of her mouth pull into a small smile as Sue smiled briefly at her. Then she blushed. She looked away, uncomfortable under Sue's scrutiny.

"My name is Sue Dobson," she continued. "I'm the RA of the house. I know most of you lived in the dorms last year, so you know what a resident adviser is. For those who don't, let me explain.

"I wear several hats here. First and foremost, I want you to know I'm here for you for anything. And I mean anything." She looked back at Tulley.

Tulley wondered why this Sue woman kept staring at her. She was paying attention. Did Sue think she wasn't?

Sue went on. "If you need help with classes, homework, ideas, you're welcome to come to me. If you need advice on something, even something not school related, come to me. If you just need an ear to bend or a shoulder to cry on, I'm here.

"On the flipside, I'm the enforcer." She smiled, and the whole room lit up. "Seriously, it's my job to make sure the rules of the house are being followed. And speaking of rules, now would be a good time to go over them with you.

"No guys. No exceptions." She paused for the anticipated groans and was not disappointed. "Same thing with alcohol and drugs. Not allowed. No exceptions.

"Obviously, we're all adults here, but we do ask you show respect for your housemates. Please be courteous and considerate of the rest of us and don't come stumbling in making a racket in the wee hours of the morning."

They sat quietly, seeming to hang on her words.

Livie leaned and whispered to Tulley, "I wonder how many times Danielle will just *have* to stay with some guy because she couldn't make it home at a reasonable hour."

Kelly overheard and snickered. Tulley smiled. Until Sue looked over and arched an eyebrow.

"Is everything okay over there?"

Kelly and Liv laughed, but Tulley could only blush and nod.

"Good. Okay, that covers the basics. Now let's talk about food. We have the main two refrigerators in the kitchen. The white one contains food for meals. That one is off limits. No snacking from that one, even if it's midnight and you've just gotten home with a wicked case of the munchies. The silver one has snacks provided for you. You're also welcome to put other food in there. Just be sure to label it. And yes, there are repercussions for letting your food go bad. And for taking your sisters' food. Be respectful and responsible. You'll hear that a lot. Be respectful and responsible. There are thirty of us living in this house, since we have members from the last two pledge classes. We don't need pettiness or attitudes. I want each of you to think about that for a minute. Ask yourself how you can avoid issues with your sisters based on attitude and then promise to do that."

The room was silent, and Tulley immediately thought of Danielle and her attitude. She knew she'd get tired of it but made a silent promise to herself to try not to let Danielle get to her. She looked back to the front of the room and saw Sue smiling at her. The woman was starting to annoy her.

"Okay, back to the food rules," Sue said. "There's another refrigerator in the game room for your use, and you're allowed to have dorm refrigerators in your rooms. We expect roommates to handle any sharing issues. The one rule for all refrigerators is no alcohol may be in them. And we can check the ones in your room anytime we'd like. Don't try to claim invasion of privacy.

"That's about it. Dinner is served at six o'clock. You're paying for it, so you might as well be here for it. You've got about an hour before dinner now. Any questions?"

No one said a word, so Sue dismissed the girls, armed with the rules and regulations of their new residence.

❖

"I could fall asleep right here in your car," Tulley told her classmate Gaby as she rested her head on the back of the passenger seat.

"What a great study session, though, right? I mean, we've already got a strong foundation for our presentation."

Tulley opened an eye and looked at Gaby sitting behind the steering wheel. She took in the ebony skin, the short, magenta dreadlocks, huge loop earrings, and pierced eyebrow. Gaby amazed her.

"But, Gaby, we each have a billion other classes to study for, too."

"And we'll study for them. But this is women's studies, and it's my favorite. Don't worry. I don't expect you to neglect your other homework. But I will definitely bug you to make sure we get this project right."

Tulley reached for the door. "Well, thanks for the ride."

"Do you live here?" Gaby asked.

"Yeah. Why?"

"This is a sorority house." She laughed.

"I know, I know."

"You're in a sorority? You don't seem the type."

"I'm not really. It's a long story," she said, not sure even she knew what she was talking about.

Gaby shook her head. "I don't get it, but I don't judge. Besides, you're surrounded by all your sisters, right?"

Tulley felt like she was missing something in the way Gaby laughed, but she grinned anyway and climbed out of the car.

"You want to get together later for something to eat?" Gaby called after her.

She thought briefly that dinner away from the house would be nice, but she decided that downtime would be better. "No thanks. Not tonight."

"Okay then. I'll see you tomorrow. Don't forget about the noon rally on the square. It'll be a great way for you to get out and meet more people. You said that was your goal this year."

"I did and it is. I'm looking forward to the rally. I'll see you then."

She crossed the parking lot and walked in the back door.

Sue had taken the first two days of the week off to make herself available as classes started for the new semester. At least that's what she told everyone. The truth was, she was hoping for a chance to get to know Tulley Stephens a bit better. Tulley intrigued her. Sue was sure Tulley was a lesbian, but she wasn't sure Tulley had figured it out. She knew it was none of her business, but Tulley was too cute to ignore.

Sue leaned on the kitchen counter and watched Tulley get out of the car. As the car turned out of the driveway, Sue spotted the telltale rainbow sticker on the bumper. She felt a pang of jealousy but quickly shook it off as she left her post and sat on her bed with a book, waiting for Tulley.

"Hey, you," she called and waited for Tulley to poke her head in her room. "How was your day?"

"Exhausting."

"Really?" She patted the bed next to her. "Come. Sit. Tell me about it."

Tulley set her book bag on the floor and looked around Sue's tiny room. The only chair had books piled high on it so she sat on the edge of the bed

"Scoot back here with me. Get comfortable. You just finished your first day."

Tulley leaned back on an elbow and looked at Sue.

"It was brutal," she said.

Sue couldn't hold her curiosity. She'd hear about the rest of Tulley's classes if she had to, but first she had to know.

"Was that a friend of yours who brought you home?" she asked.

"Who? Gaby? No. Well, yeah now. She's in my women's studies class. She connected with me in class, and afterward, we went to the library to start working on our project that's not due till November. But she's all over it."

"Do you have a group you're working with?"

"No. It's just the two of us. But that's cool because she's easy to work with. And she's focused."

"Good for you." Sue relaxed a bit. She didn't get the sense Tulley was all that into this Gaby woman.

"I know. But she's into women's studies. I mean, I like learning about women who really brought it over history and all, but she's like obsessed with it. I'm supposed to go to some rally tomorrow. She wants me to meet people." She groaned. "I don't do well at meeting people."

Sue smiled at her. "You'll be fine. Why does she want you to meet people?"

"I don't know. She thinks I need to come out of my shell. I know I'm a loner, for the most part, but that works for me."

Sue's heart melted for Tulley. She was adorable, shy, and clueless. And she had a pretty good feeling it wasn't her shell Gaby wanted Tulley to come out of.

"Well, maybe you'll meet people with some common interests. You never know."

Tulley looked at her doubtfully.

"I mean it," Sue said. "Maybe some of them will have a lot in common with you and you'll have some new people to hang out with, even if it's just in between classes. Or they might introduce you to more interests."

"You can try to convince me of whatever you want, but it's gonna suck. Not that it matters. I've already committed to it and I don't think Gaby would be too happy if I blew her off."

"What if I went with you?" The words were out of Sue's mouth before she could engage her brain-to-mouth filter.

"Do you mean that?"

"Sure. I was hoping to stop by there anyway. This way, you'd at least know someone there. I mean, besides Gaby."

"That would be cool." Tulley sounded hesitant. "So you're interested in women's issues, too?"

"Don't you think all women should be?"

"I do now. I never thought about it before." She stood and grabbed her book bag. "I need to go study."

"Okay, I'll see you at dinner."

After dinner, several members were relaxing in the front room watching television. Danielle and several of her friends were on the long couch against the front wall. Mindy, Kelly, and Livie were on another. Tulley sat on the floor in front of theirs, leaning back into it.

During a commercial break, Sue walked up and stood over Tulley. "We didn't pick a meeting place tomorrow. How does the student union at quarter of sound?"

"That sounds great. Thanks."

As soon as Sue was out of earshot, Danielle said snidely, "Was that a date?"

Tulley's group looked at her. "What?"

"A date. I mean, you and Sue would make a cute couple, don't you think?"

Her friends snickered and Tulley's blood boiled. She knew she was about to lose control, so she stormed out of the room. She was lying on her bed when Livie came in.

"Why do you let her get to you? She only says that shit to piss you off."

"Well, it works."

"If you're not gay, it shouldn't matter, and if you are…well, if you are, it shouldn't matter, either. It's nobody's business."

"But I'm not gay!" Tulley blurted.

"Is everything okay?" Sue called from the door, her heart sinking at what she'd just overheard. "I heard there were some words exchanged downstairs."

"We're fine," Tulley said. "I'm gonna study some more and go to sleep. I'll see you guys tomorrow."

Sue walked downstairs feeling like any progress Tulley had made had just been washed down the drain. She hoped she could point her in the right direction again. She, of all people, knew that a closet was a suffocating place to live.

Chapter Seven

Sue and Tulley made their way around the plaza, marveling at the plethora of information offered at the multitude of booths. It was a warm August day with a clear blue sky and Sue was more than happy to have Tulley to herself for a few minutes.

"I'm surprised your friend hasn't found you yet," Sue said.

"There are a lot of people here. She'll find us."

As if on cue, Gaby walked up and wrapped her arms around Tulley. "I'm so glad you made it!"

Sue couldn't help her reaction. She was filled with jealousy. She wanted her arms around Tulley. Her only consolation was the unmistakable look of discomfort on Tulley's face.

As Tulley managed to disengage herself from Gaby, Gaby looked at Sue. With no attempt to hide dislike for her, she said, "I don't think we've met."

"This is my…friend, Sue," Tulley said.

Gaby squinted at her as she seemed to ponder the delay.

Sue decidedly did not like the possessiveness Gaby was displaying. Much as she wanted to slap her, she decided to play nice. She extended her hand. "Hi. Nice to meet you."

Gaby placed a limp hand in hers. Sue fought a smirk. She liked that the intruder was threatened by her. What she didn't like was that it meant she was hell-bent on turning Tulley.

"Thanks for bringing her," Gaby said dismissively. "I'll show her around now."

Sue saw the way Tulley's glance went from her to Gaby and back. She could feel the tension radiating from her. She looked like she wanted to get away from everything—the crowd and Gaby and Sue.

"We could all walk around together," Tulley said.

Gaby looked at her like she'd forgotten she was there.

"That'll work," Sue said, not about to give Gaby any more alone time with Tulley than she had to.

"Let's go this way first." Gaby grabbed Tulley's arm, pulling her in the opposite direction from Sue.

Sue shook her head and grinned, thinking poor Gaby had no idea she had met her match. She let her anger go and decided to relax and enjoy herself, hopefully at Gaby's expense.

The first booth Gaby dragged them to was promoting better rights for immigrant workers. She picked up a clipboard.

"Have you seen the workers in the orchards around here?" Gaby asked, staring intently into Tulley's eyes. "They're expected to work up to sixteen hours a day, and they pay them horribly. Not to mention the conditions. And if one of the workers gets hurt, that's their problem, not the orchard owner's. You should sign this petition to give them better rights."

Sue took the clipboard quickly before Gaby could react. She pretended to study it as she asked Tulley, "Hey, kiddo, don't your parents use immigrants on their vineyard?"

Tulley edged behind her and read over her shoulder. "Yeah."

"Do they treat them the way Gaby described?"

"No. They treat them well. They're known for treating their employees fairly. I'm kind of proud of that. They don't differentiate between employees. Locals and immigrants are all treated the same."

"Well, not everyone is like that," Gaby said defensively. "You should still sign the petition. Everyone should be treated fairly."

"What exactly are we signing for?" Sue refused to let Gaby box her out. "I mean, it wouldn't force Tulley's parents into changing the way they do anything, would it? Do you know the details?"

Gaby grabbed it back. "Obviously, I don't know every last detail. But I know everyone deserves equal rights."

"Maybe we should stick to booths concerning women's issues," Sue suggested.

"Yeah," Tulley seemed quick to agree. "That's what I'm really into learning about now, and I only have an hour until my next class."

"Let's go see what's this way." Sue led her down another row of booths, leaving Gaby standing there holding the clipboard. "Do you see any booth you want to check out?"

"I think I'd rather walk around and see what kind of things are here. I'm not ready to jump in and rally. That's not me, you know?" She laughed.

"That's fine." They turned to see Gaby had caught up. "We can take it as slowly as you need to."

Sue looked at Tulley, who apparently missed the double entendre. "That's a good idea."

Out of the corner of her eye, Sue spotted the table of the Fenton State Lesbian Organization. She wondered how Tulley would react to the group. By slightly crowding her as they walked along, she managed to steer her to the table.

"Check this out," she said.

The three women at the table stood to greet them. The two femmes were practically drooling over Tulley, while the butch struck up a conversation with Sue.

"We're having a meeting this Thursday," a petite blond femme told Tulley as she handed her a flier. "You should try to be there."

Sue turned to see her response and saw Gaby do the same.

Tulley held the flier in her hand. Sue tried to decipher the smile on her face.

"I can't make it Thursday," Tulley said. "But I have to tell you I think your organization is pretty cool. It's great that there's a place where people can be comfortable being out."

The girl talking to her wrote her name, number, and e-mail address on a piece of paper and handed it to Tulley. "If you want any more info about us, or anything really, you can get a hold of me here."

She handed another piece of paper to Tulley. "Why don't you write down your info for us?"

Tulley stared at the paper, then took a pen from the table and jotted her name and number. She was there to make new friends, and these girls seemed nice enough. She hesitated before handing it over.

"I live in a house," she began, "with lots of roommates. I don't always have the privacy to talk, so if I don't answer, just leave me a message."

She turned and looked at Sue, hoping she wasn't offended that she hadn't admitted she lived in a sorority house. Something inside told her the girls wouldn't like her as much if they knew. And their liking her was important.

When Sue smiled at her, she felt warm all over, like she had her approval. She didn't question why that was so important to her either; she simply enjoyed the feeling as she handed the paper to the girl at the booth.

"It's no biggie. I'm not afraid of voice mail"

Sue watched the interaction with interest. Tulley seemed comfortable. That was a good sign. She watched Gaby watch the interaction, too, and knew it was killing her that the two lesbians were openly flirting with Tulley. What Sue couldn't figure out was how she felt about Tulley's actions.

Other women had approached the booth so they stepped back out of the way.

"They seemed nice enough," Sue said.

"You would think so," Gaby said. "The way that one was all over you."

"Who was all over you?" Tulley quickly asked.

"That tall, dark, and handsome butch," Gaby sad. "You can't tell me you didn't notice. Or maybe those other girls held your attention."

"Well, I was talking to them and not really watching the other one."

They walked on for a few minutes, and Sue asked if any other booths might interest her.

"Actually, a lot of them do, but like I said, I'm not ready to jump in. I have some ideas of what's out there. I'll think about things and then contact whatever groups I decide on."

"Good idea," Sue said.

"And if you have any questions about any of them, you can let me know," Gaby said. "I'll help you make up your mind."

"Thanks," Tulley said, not quite sure if she meant it. She liked Gaby but realized she could be a little overbearing. "For now, I need to get to class. Thank you both for hanging with me. Gaby, I'll see you in class tomorrow. Sue, I'll see you tonight."

After she walked off, Sue turned to leave.

"She'll see you tonight?" Gaby asked.

"That's what she said." And without further explanation, Sue turned and began her walk back to the house.

❖

Tulley was happy to get back to the house after her day. Her classes weren't difficult, especially since the last three teachers had only handed out their syllabi. She was still on edge from her walk in the square. While she had hoped she'd feel more comfortable with Sue there, she had felt worse.

She let herself in the back door and saw Sue in her room putting on makeup.

"Thanks again for going with me today," Tulley said.

"No problem. Did you have fun?"

Tulley watched her working in front of her tabletop mirror. She hadn't considered Sue the makeup type.

"It was okay. I told you I don't do people that well."

"You were fine. I'd never have guessed it."

"Why are you getting all dolled up?" she blurted before she realized what she'd said.

"I'm going out."

"Oh."

Sue turned to face her. "That's okay with you, isn't it?" She smiled.

"Sure." Tulley felt a slight blush creep over her face. Before she could feel any less comfortable, her phone rang.

"I should take this."

"I suppose you should."

Relieved, she stepped out of Sue's room and answered the phone.

"Hello?"

"Hey, Tull, it's Gaby."

"What's up?"

"I just wondered if you wanted to go grab a beer and maybe shoot some pool."

"Where?"

"A bar I know."

"A bar where we can get served? Is it The Asylum?"

"I don't know that one. How about I swing by and pick you up around eight?"

"Sounds good."

Gaby arrived right on time and headed her car toward town.

"I haven't spent a lot of time in bars outside of the campus area. How did you find out about the one we're going to?"

"A friend took me last year."

"You sure they'll serve us?"

Gaby glanced over at Tulley. "I have no doubt we'll get served."

Tulley was happy to hear that as she relaxed into the passenger seat. She was very happy Gaby had befriended her. While Gaby was nineteen, the same as her, she seemed so worldly. She seemed to live outside of the college realm. Normally, that wouldn't sit well with Tulley, but she trusted Gaby and felt she could allow her to lead her to new adventures.

She was more than a little surprised when Gaby parked the car in front of some sort of pet grooming store.

"What are we doing here?"

Gaby laughed. "The bar's in the back. Trust me."

Tulley followed her into the building, around a counter, and through a dark curtain that led to a large room with an open layout. There was a bar along one wall, a dance floor bordered by tables where a few women sat chatting, and a couple pool tables in a raised area along the far wall.

She briefly noted that both pool tables were being used as she and Gaby stepped up to the bar and ordered their beers.

"Did you want to go put some quarters on the tables?" Gaby asked, motioning toward the raised area.

"No, let's just chill for a while." She sat at a table and took in her surroundings again.

"Does this place ever fill up?"

"Oh, yeah. On weekends, it's wall to wall."

Tulley couldn't imagine. It seemed cavernous and empty. There was also something about the place that seemed different, but she couldn't put her finger on it.

"You okay?"

"Yeah. Just checking things out."

"I bet you are."

"What?"

"Nothing." Gaby smiled before taking a swallow of beer. "Not a damned thing."

❖

Sue was enjoying her evening at the Top Cat with Jo. She was all worked up after spending time with Tulley. She had been wet and swollen since walking around campus with her. She knew she should curtail her crush on her, but she couldn't help it. Besides, it was harmless. Who knew if Tulley was ever going to figure things out?

For now, she'd continue to fantasize about her in bed at night, pretending her battery-operated tongue was Tulley working magic between her legs. And when it got really bad, like that particular night, she was pretty sure she could find someone to ease the aching desire.

Jo had just broken a particularly passionate kiss when a new couple entering the bar caught Sue's eye. She stopped, her glass of white wine halfway to her mouth. It was Gaby and Tulley. Sue didn't know which felt worse, the fact that her sexuality might be exposed or that Gaby seemed to have the upper hand in the quest for Tulley. And then another thought hit. Was it possible that Tulley was aware of her proclivities and had been playing innocent at the house?

She stepped back to remain hidden as Gaby and Tulley took their table. The way Tulley was looking around, it didn't appear that she'd been there before. That was a good sign. Gaby was grinning like the cat that had swallowed the canary. Sue's blood boiled. Gaby was pushing Tulley too fast. It wasn't fair to her. Not that Sue could do anything about it if she was going to make sure Tulley didn't know she was there. Or maybe it was too late.

Tulley continued to process her surroundings, still trying to register what was different. There was music in the background, coming from the jukebox on the far wall. The walls were brick, the floor hardwood. It was scuffed everywhere but the dance floor, which shone. She saw two women emerge from the hallway holding hands, and the light bulb went off. She quickly looked at each patron and realized there wasn't a man in the place.

Did Gaby think she was like that? She had no problems with lesbians, but she wasn't one. The last thing she wanted was for Gaby to think she was into her as more than just a friend.

Tulley couldn't look at her. She wondered what Gaby's expectations were after taking her to a bar like that. She looked anywhere but across the table at her. She decided to act like she was engrossed in the pool games, even though she could barely see the balls due to the angle.

"Are you looking for her?" Gaby asked.

"Who?" Tulley looked back at her.

"Your friend up there."

She turned back to the pool tables and for a brief second, thought she saw Sue. If it wasn't, it was a woman who looked remarkably like her. Her heart skipped a beat even as the woman stepped back, blocked from view by the other women.

"I'm not sure that was her." She faced Gaby again.

"I'm pretty sure it is. I've seen her here before."

Another light bulb flashed in Tulley's mind. They were both lesbians? Could it be they were both interested in her? She couldn't imagine, but it would sure explain the animosity earlier.

"So you knew who she was when you saw her this afternoon?"

"I wasn't sure. But I saw her here just now and I knew. She's always up there when she comes here. She's not a regular or anything, but when she does stop by, she hangs out at the pool tables and leaves with the tall, dark one."

Tulley watched as the woman in question, wearing tight black jeans and a tighter black muscle shirt, stepped away from the table and walked over to where she'd last seen Sue behind the crowd. She saw the dark woman bend her head and lean her body into the wall. But Tulley knew it wasn't the wall at all. As the woman's hips began to grind, Tulley thought her head would explode. How dare she kiss Sue like that?

Gaby laughed. "You look jealous, sister."

Tulley could feel the heat on her neck and face. She was embarrassed to have been caught staring.

"Not jealous. I just didn't realize she was gay."

"You really had no idea?"

"None. I didn't know you were, either."

She tried to read Gaby's thoughts behind the dark pools that were her eyes. She thought she saw distrust, disbelief, and maybe a touch of pity.

"What?" she asked defensively.

"Nothing. I just find it hard to believe your gaydar doesn't work."

"My gaydar? You're kidding, right?"

"You don't think you have gaydar?"

"Yeah, no. I don't think so." She was growing more uncomfortable by the moment. "You know what? I think it's time to get home. I've got studying to do," she lied.

"Aw, come on. So she's kissing someone. It doesn't mean we can't have another beer."

"Seriously, I need to get going. Thanks for the beer and I'll buy next time, but I should get home."

They drove back to the house in silence, Tulley lost in thoughts about Gaby and Sue. Was it true the only reason they were nice to her was because they *liked* her, liked her? Questioning Sue's feelings for her, she wasn't sure she ever wanted to see her again but wasn't sure how she could avoid her for the rest of the year.

❖

Sue couldn't believe Jo's kiss. She desperately wanted to know if Tulley had seen it. If she had, there was no way she could explain she just happened to be at a lesbian bar. At the same time, if she had, well, something about that got Sue really hot.

"We need to get out of here," she whispered to Jo. "I need you. Now."

They snuck out the back door and crossed to Jo's truck. Sue lay back and pulled Jo on top of her, wrapping her legs around her to press Jo's hips into her crotch while she kissed her, plunging her tongue deep in Jo's mouth.

"Easy, girl." Jo laughed against her lips. "Hold that thought till we get to the garage."

When they were safely inside, Sue immediately stripped. "I want the biggest dildo you have. Strap it on. I need everything you can give me."

Jo grinned and unlocked her special toolbox. When her harness was on just right, she chose a red tool with a wide girth and locked it in place. She looked at Sue.

"Lay down. I want to ride that cock till I cream all over it." Even Sue was amazed at the pure carnal lust raging through her.

But her fear of being outed by Tulley turned into arousal that Tulley might have seen Jo kissing her. As she straddled Jo and moved up and down on the hard rod, she fantasized Tulley had been jealous and fought Jo for her. That Tulley prevailed and claimed her, taking her home and making love to her in a way she deserved. The fantasy reached its peak right as Sue climaxed, her body quivering until she fell onto Jo's chest, completely drained.

CHAPTER EIGHT

"Tulley!" Sue called as Tulley raced past her room the next day.

Tulley paused briefly, debated turning back, but decided against it. Instead, she picked up her pace and darted around the corner and up the stairs. She put her book bag down and lay on her bed, covering her eyes with her arm. She wasn't ready to deal with Sue. It had been hard enough to avoid Gaby after class. She knew living in the same house as Sue would make it close to impossible to avoid her.

"We need to talk," Sue said softly from the doorway, causing Tulley to start.

"Why?" Tulley didn't look at her, so Sue sat on Livie's bed.

"I'm not sure where to start."

"Probably because there's nothing to be said."

"I know you saw me last night. And now you know I saw you."

Tulley felt ice in the pit of her stomach.

"Now do you agree we have something to talk about?"

Tulley sat up. "I didn't know what kind of bar it was until we were there. Gaby just said she knew a bar where we could get served. I wasn't there because I'm gay, and I wasn't there because I knew you were there."

The last statement caught Sue off guard. She'd never even considered that option.

"It doesn't matter why you were there."

"It does to me. Gaby took me there because she thinks I'm a lesbian. Now I know why you've been so nice to me. You think I'm one, too."

"That's not true—"

"Really?" She shook her head. "You know, I honestly thought you and Gaby liked me. Like as a friend. Not because you thought I might be interested in you."

"I would be lying if I told you I didn't find you attractive. But I've befriended you because I can tell you're uncomfortable here. I don't know why you pledged, but you did. And now you live in this house feeling like an outcast. That's why I decided to make friends with you.

"It's my job to help new members' transitions into living at the house happen as seamlessly as possible. That's the way it started with you. But it's more. I like you and enjoy talking to you. That's why I'm nice to you. I have no ulterior motive."

"So if I came out to you right now, you would walk away and not even consider making a move on me?"

"That's not what this conversation is about."

"You're not answering me."

"You're not really coming out to me."

"So what is this about then?"

"My original point was that we were both at the Top Cat last night. You realize that could cause major problems for us if anyone found out."

"You're not out?"

Sue shook her head. "You've heard Danielle. Every pledge class has members like that. And the old-timers are worse. I made a promise to myself when I pledged to stay closeted as long as I was active."

"But you were at a gay bar."

"I'm out in the outer world. I go places where I'm pretty certain I won't be seen. Obviously, it never occurred to me that I'd see someone from the sorority at the bar."

"So what did you come up here to talk to me about if you don't want to congratulate me for being part of the club?"

"I need to make sure you understand that if anyone finds out we were there, it could be a major problem for both of us."

"You don't have to worry about me. I won't say a word."

"Good." Sue stood to leave, then looked down at Tulley. "And for the record, you don't have to be a lesbian to enjoy a women's bar."

❖

Tulley lay in bed that night thinking of the past two days and everything that had happened. Her thoughts took her back to her high school softball days and Coach Peters, one of the only adults she'd ever felt comfortable around. Coach had always said that everything happened for a reason and that sometimes you had to look harder to see the reasons. And sometimes you had to clear your mind and let the reasons show themselves to you.

Her head hurt from all the thinking she'd been doing, so she lay on her back and forced herself to clear her mind. Like Coach had taught her, she released her thoughts and concerns to the cosmos and asked that explanations be shown to her.

As she lay there, the silence was broken by sounds coming from the bunk above her. At first, there were simply low moans, but soon the noises got louder, leaving no doubt what Kelly was doing above her. When the mattress started bouncing, Tulley bolted from the room before Kelly could embarrass them both. She glanced back at Livie, who was still sound asleep, before making her way down the dark stairs to the kitchen.

Sue was reading in bed when the kitchen light went on. Curious who it was, she put her book down and got up to investigate.

She stopped in the doorway when she saw Tulley in her pajama pants and T-shirt taking milk from the refrigerator. She admired the sight before her—the way the shirt clung to the small, firm breasts and taut stomach, the way her pajama bottoms rode low on her boyish hips. Sue thought of several things she'd like to do to her.

"What are you doing up?" Sue asked.

"Getting something to drink."

"Don't you keep milk in the fridge in your room?"

"I couldn't sleep. My dad always used to give me warm milk to help me sleep."

"Your dad? Not your mom, huh? Are you and your dad close?"

"Very."

"Why can't you sleep?" Sue took the milk and motioned to the kitchen table.

After a brief pause, Tulley said, "Kelly is talking in her sleep."

"What a pain. I don't miss roommates." She grabbed the vanilla and cinnamon from the cabinet.

"How did you end up as the RA? Wouldn't you rather live somewhere else? Where you can be, you know, free?"

"You mean out?"

"Well, sure. But also no curfews or anything. Haven't you ever wanted to live somewhere besides the house?"

"I've thought about it. But then I'd have to get a real job. And I like being able to concentrate most of my time and effort on school."

She handed the cup to Tulley and sat with her. She tried not to be obvious as she admired her again. Even in the middle of the night, her blue eyes were bright and shone with life. She watched her soft lips part slightly as she took a sip of milk. And she felt the twitch between her legs as Tulley licked the remnants off.

"This is really good. Thank you."

"No problem. Just don't let anyone know I aided and abetted a curfew breaker."

Tulley laughed; an easy sound that made Sue relax.

"So we're good, right?"

"What? Oh, yeah. We're fine."

"Good. Then finish up and we'll go to bed."

Tulley looked questioningly at Sue.

"Not like that." Sue reached out to pat her hand. "Not that way."

"I knew that." Tulley's laugh sounded forced. "I knew that."

She drained her cup and let Sue take it from her to rinse.

"Thanks again. I feel much better," she said, but Sue wasn't convinced.

Tulley lay in bed listening to the soft, easy breathing of her roommates. She wished sleep would come to her, but she couldn't settle her mind. Her thoughts kept going back to Sue. Her feelings were jumbled. Finding out Sue was a lesbian wasn't an issue for her in a political way. Yet she couldn't stop thinking about it. Her thoughts meandered to the woman she'd seen Sue with at the Top Cat. This time, the tightening of her stomach wasn't due to nerves. She recognized it as the same feeling she'd had the first time she saw her best friend from high school kissing Zack Mendez. She had a feeling her world was about to change yet again.

CHAPTER NINE

Thursday night found the house a bustle of activity as the women of Gamma Alpha Epsilon prepared themselves for their social with the men of Alpha Sigma Pi. The theme was "Rock Stars of the 1980s." Danielle waltzed down the hall looking like a slutty Madonna. Livie was dressed as Pat Benatar, while Kelly opted for the Debbie Harry look.

They all began to congregate in the front room, laughing and talking and waiting to go to the fraternity house together. Tulley wrapped a purple-striped scarf around her neck like a tie, put her fake guitar in place, and checked herself out in the mirror. Her tight red pants and striped shirt unbuttoned to her navel made her look the part perfectly. The cheap dark wig she wore topped off the ensemble. She felt good as she joined her sisters downstairs.

Livie and Kelly laughed when they saw her.

"That's perfect," Kelly told her.

"I love it," Livie said.

"Thanks. I think it turned out pretty well."

Danielle sauntered over with her groupies in tow. She flipped Tulley's tie.

"Just who the hell are you supposed to be?"

"Eddie Van Halen."

"He's a guy."

"So what? He was an eighties rock star."

"You had to be a guy. You are such a dyke." She turned around, as did the rest of her cronies after giving Tulley the once-over.

"Don't let them get to you," Kelly said.

"You know what?" Tulley said. "I won't. I'm dressed up in theme as someone I like, and it doesn't matter what they think."

Livie hugged her, making Tulley's bravado slip a bit. But she kept it together, determined to drink beer, have fun, and forget reality for a while.

❖

Sue sat on the couch watching the young women milling about. She smiled when she saw Tulley come downstairs, thinking how adorable she was. She held back when Danielle verbally attacked Tulley but was on standby in case she needed to step in. By the time the older actives got there so everyone could walk together, Sue was more than ready for some peace and quiet. She had a project to work on and was looking forward to a silent house in which to get it done.

She stood and said good-bye, helping everyone to the door and out to enjoy the evening. She caught Tulley's eye and smiled briefly before looking away, not wanting to cause any further confusion or trouble for her.

❖

Dance music was blaring as the group arrived and stood in front of the frat house. On the ground leading to the right of the house were replicas of the covers of some of the greatest albums of the eighties. They followed the trail of *Thriller* by Michael Jackson, *Shake it Up* by The Cars, *Brothers in Arms* by Dire Straits, *The Completion Backward Principle* by The Tubes, *1999* by Prince, and others around to the backyard where the men of ASP cheered their arrival. They raised their beer cups and directed the women toward the keg.

Tulley was amused at the number of frat boys who were dressed so similarly to Danielle. And most looked better. She, Kelly, and Livie followed the press of their sisters and gladly accepted cups of beer from the fraternity pledge manning the keg.

"Did you see how he looked at you?" Livie asked her.

"What?" Tulley looked back and saw the keg boy still looking at her. She looked away quickly but not before he managed to flash a dimpled smile at her. He had on jeans and a plain white T-shirt like the rest of the pledges. His dark hair was short and wavy, and he smiled like he knew he was cute.

"He is way cute," Kelly said.

"And he knows it," Tulley yelled over the music.

"Still…" Livie giggled.

They moved out of the crowd and stood back, drinking their beer and watching the rest of the group mingle. They watched a circle open in the middle of the crowd as the sound system began blasting music that matched the theme of the party. People immediately started jumping up and down with their arms pinned to their sides as Devo told them to "Whip It."

"I'm gonna get another beer," Tulley said as she drained her cup.

"Already?" Kelly looked down at hers, still over half full.

"I'm thirsty," Tulley called over her shoulder.

"Wow, you sure pounded your beer," the cute keg boy said.

Tulley blushed but didn't answer. She took her beer from him and walked back to her friends. Or where they had been. They weren't where she'd left them. She looked around and eventually saw them dancing to "Love Shack."

"I brought you another beer," a loud voice said in her ear.

She turned and saw the dark-haired young man standing next to her.

"I just got this one," she said.

"So drink fast."

Tulley did as she was instructed and accepted the next one.

"My name's Joey."

"Tulley."

"Cool name. Hey, you want something real to drink?"

"Like what?"

Joey pulled a flask out of his back pocket and handed it to her. She unscrewed the top and sniffed. The powerful smell of tequila assaulted her nostrils.

"I think I burned my nose hairs," she said, handing it back.

He pushed her hand toward her mouth. "Oh, come on. Take a drink. It tastes better than it smells, I promise."

Still wary but feeling bold, Tulley took a long pull of the potent liquid. She felt it trail a warm path down her throat and settle in her stomach. Her head immediately felt lighter.

"Take another drink," Joey said.

This time, Tulley tilted her head back and took two large swallows before handing the flask back to him. She chased them with several gulps of beer and was starting to relax.

"You wanna dance?"

"I don't dance."

"Why not?"

"I don't like to."

"Has anyone ever told you that you're cute, Tulley?"

She stared hard at him, determined to ascertain whether he was sincere or not. She knew frat boys loved to use lines like that. She decided he really thought so and blushed again.

"No."

"You're kidding, right? Because you are."

"Thanks. So are you."

The music had slowed and Air Supply was crooning over the loudspeakers.

"Come on. How about just one dance?"

Her mind growing foggier every moment, Tulley couldn't remember why she didn't like dancing to begin with. And Joey was such a nice boy.

"Okay. We can dance."

She let him take her hand and lead her to the dance floor. She was having a hard time maintaining her balance and was grateful when she felt Joey's arms around her. She leaned into him more to stabilize herself than for anything.

As they moved, Joey pulled her closer and pressed into her. She felt his hands moving along her back as they worked their way lower. One of them barely grazed her left butt cheek and she thought about moving away, but it was brief, so she reasoned it had probably been an accident.

When she felt his lips on her neck, she knew that couldn't have been an accident. She pulled away briefly, but before she could say anything, he closed the distance and kissed her. His kiss wasn't as sloppy as the boy's at the flower pinning, but it was still too forceful for her. She barely had time to register that his mouth was on hers when she felt his tongue prying her lips apart. At the same time, she felt a hand close over her breast.

She recoiled in disgust and stumbled backward. Right into Danielle, who had been dancing behind her.

"What is your problem?"

Tulley stared at her, the words slowly sinking in. She felt Joey grab her arm but pulled away and forced herself to run on rubbery legs out of the party.

A block from the house, Tulley sat on the curb and tried to clear her head. She was dizzy and confused. She recognized she'd had too much tequila too fast, but she hadn't expected it to kick her ass that hard. As she sat there taking deep breaths of fresh air, she admitted to herself she had come very close to letting Joey take advantage of her. Just because he was cute, he thought he had the right to her. She'd had no interest in him. She searched her memory and could find nothing she'd said or done to give him the impression she liked him.

Feeling a little better and with a clearer head, Tulley stood and tested her legs. They felt stronger, so she walked the rest of the way to the sorority house.

Sue started at the sound of the front door closing. She wasn't expecting anybody and the social should have just been warming up. She walked out of the kitchen to see Tulley walking toward the stairs.

"Hey, kiddo. Is everything okay?"

"Yeah. I kind of had too much to drink."

"Already?"

"Look, I know I was stupid. You don't need to rub it in."

Sue was torn. She had her work spread all over the kitchen table and needed to get the project done. Tulley was defensive. If Sue'd learned one thing about her it was that defensive usually meant she was in pain.

"I'm not rubbing anything in. Why don't you come into the kitchen with me and we'll talk?"

Tulley looked at her, then walked over and slumped onto a couch, staring at her feet.

Sue sat next to her. "So what happened?"

"I told you," Tulley said remorsefully. "I drank too much."

Sue could smell booze on Tulley's breath. "Where did you get the tequila?"

Tulley looked at her. "You can tell?"

"You reek."

"One of their pledges had a flask of it. I had a few drinks from it. And I drank like three beers really fast, too."

"You know, you've had a rough week. It's not surprising for you to overdo it tonight. Although I have to say you don't seem that drunk to me."

"I sure felt it earlier. It hit me hard. Then I was dancing with him and he kissed me and I pulled away and that's when I realized I was drunk."

Sue tried to stay calm as she absorbed what Tulley was saying. She knew what happened at parties. It was common practice for the boys to see how drunk they could get the girls in hopes they'd be able to score. Still, she was very protective of Tulley and her blood boiled at the prospect of someone hurting her.

"I'm sorry that happened. I'm glad you got out of there before things got too far."

"Me too." She was silent for a long moment.

"What are you thinking?" Sue asked.

"I don't know. Maybe I overreacted. I mean, Joey was really cute."

Sue was at a loss, the statement having come out of left field. "What's that got to do with anything? If he kissed you and you didn't want him to, you had every right to pull away. Don't ever feel you owe these guys anything."

"Maybe I should have let it go, though, and seen where it would end up."

"Tulley, let me ask you something. Did his kiss ignite something inside you? Did it make you crave more? More kisses? His touch? Anything like that?"

"No."

"Then you did the right thing."

"What if…"

"What if what?"

Tulley hesitated briefly and then stared into Sue's eyes. "What if I just don't like guys?"

While Sue had wondered when this subject would arise, she found herself completely unprepared at that moment. Her own heart and mind battled over how to respond. Part of her wanted to hug Tulley and congratulate her for realizing who she was and encourage her to embrace it and be proud. Part of her wondered how much the pressures of the week were forcing her to move too fast. And the responsible part of her knew she had to maintain a professional distance and simply encourage Tulley to talk.

"You're the only one who would know that for sure. There's been a lot of lesbian talk this week. Maybe you're confused. Let me ask you this, have you ever questioned it before?"

Sue watched Tulley's expression change. She saw her gaze drop to Sue's lips. She briefly thought she should move away, but couldn't make herself as Tulley leaned toward her.

She felt Tulley's lips on hers and her heart rate surged. She let Tulley set the pace, tentative at first but growing bolder with each passing second. Her own passion flaring, she threw off Tulley's wig and ran her hands through her short, thick hair. The move seemed to embolden Tulley as Sue felt her tongue pressing against her lips, seeking entry.

Without hesitation, Sue opened her mouth and gladly welcomed Tulley in. The fire that had been smoldering between her legs was raging. Many nights had been spent masturbating to this fantasy. And now it was coming true. She lay back on the couch, pulling Tulley on top of her.

Tulley broke the kiss and struggled to catch her breath. Her chest was heaving as she looked down on Sue under her. She smiled.

Sue stared up at Tulley and the passion fogging her judgment lifted abruptly. Rather than the object of her desire, she was able to see a young woman who was in her charge. She couldn't begin to imagine the trouble she'd get into if this ever got out.

"Hey, Tulley?" she whispered. "Come on. We need to sit up."

Tulley's eyes slowly cleared of passion and she sat, elbows on knees and head in hands.

"You okay, kiddo?"

"I'm sorry. I thought you liked it…"

"I did. Very much. Too much."

Tulley stood and whirled to face Sue. "What's that supposed to mean?"

"I could easily have lost myself there. I did, actually. But I'm in a position of authority with you. People would say I corrupted you."

"That doesn't make any sense. How could you corrupt me? I'm the one who kissed you."

"Still, people see things how they want to. And you know how people around here love to talk."

Tulley's eyes were brimming with tears.

"Tulley?"

"I can't believe I made an ass out of myself twice in one night!" She turned and ran upstairs, taking them two at a time.

Sue fought the urge to go after her. She hoped Tulley would process things and understand. Besides, she didn't trust herself alone with Tulley in her bedroom. She knew she'd done the right thing.

CHAPTER TEN

Tulley opted not to go to class on Friday. She was too depressed to deal with life. She didn't want to leave her bed and move about the house due to her terror of running into Sue. She didn't want to be on campus because she was sure Gaby would take one look at her and know what had transpired the previous evening.

So she shut off her alarm clock and lay in bed listening to the low-key sounds of her sisters trying to get ready for school after a late night of partying. Livie and Kelly entered the room after taking their showers and sat at their respective vanities.

"Why aren't you up yet, sleepyhead? Are you hungover?" Livie laughed.

"I'm not hungover," Tulley said defensively. "I'm just not up for my first class today. I don't feel like going."

"And it's only the first week," Kelly pointed out while applying her makeup.

"Whatever. That's the point. It's only the first week," Tulley said.

"But this could be setting a very dangerous precedent," Livie said.

"Would you guys just back off?" Tulley rolled over and covered her head with her pillow.

They quit badgering her, so she rolled back to join in their conversation.

"How was the rest of the party?"

"It was a lot of fun. Joey spent all night asking us if you'd come back."

"Whatever."

"What happened?" Kelly asked quietly.

"He was a creep."

"I think he really liked you," Livie said.

"I think you're kind of naïve."

Livie walked over to her closet to examine her choice of outfits for the day. She took down a pair of coffee slacks and a beige blouse and laid them on her bed, then dropped her towel as she walked to her bureau for her underwear.

Tulley's heart raced. She stared at her naked, oblivious roommate, and sensations from her time on the couch with Sue washed over her again. She hadn't been that drunk. Now she knew without a doubt that she wanted to see Sue like that. To see her, feel her, touch her.

Afraid one of them might see her staring, she rolled over again and stared at the wall, terrified of the reactions her body was having to sights and people she'd be seeing day in and day out for the rest of the year. It was only the first week of school. She didn't think she'd be able to survive a whole year in the house. But it would cost her parents money to break the lease. And what excuse could she possibly give them for needing to move out? She had gotten herself into quite a quandary.

When she was sure she had the house to herself, she finally got out of bed and took a shower in the empty bathroom. She was enjoying the peace and quiet, the lack of bodies pressed together as they waited for a shower or stood curling or straightening their hair. It was blessedly empty for her, and she had every intention of enjoying it.

As she stepped out of her boxers and wifebeater, she felt a peculiar sense of awareness of her body. Looking around just to be sure no one was there, she stepped in front of the full-length mirror and closely scrutinized herself. She'd never paid a lot of attention to her looks. She was of medium build and in good shape. That's all she'd ever cared about. Now she picked her body apart piece by piece.

Sue liked women. So Tulley tried to think what she'd heard men liked in a woman and assumed Sue would like the same things. Boobs. Men loved boobs. The bigger, the better. Was that true with lesbians? Was it true with Sue? She looked at her perky set. They were firm and round but not very big. Was that why Sue didn't want her?

She turned so she could check out her butt. She craned her neck to see the reflection, as well as the real thing. It was neither big nor small. It was tight and sat high. Was that good? These were things she'd never considered and knew she'd worry about incessantly now.

Turning back around, she examined her breasts anew. She ran her hands over them before squeezing them together. The sensation caused a quick intake of breath. She pinched her hardening nipples, imagining it was Sue paying them attention. A powerful current ran straight to her core.

She closed her eyes and reveled in the feeling. She imagined touching Sue like this and Sue touching her. Sue touching her won out, and she held that thought as she quit squeezing and began to tug and twist at her nipples. Just a little at first, to provide pressure and let her pleasure center come to attention. As she pinched the tips of them harder and pictured Sue's mouth on them, her pussy clenched and she moaned.

Remembering where she was, she quickly locked the bathroom doors. If anyone else was in the house, let them be pissed. She needed release.

Tulley sat on the bench that ran the length of the wall across from the floor-length mirror and continued to play with her nipples. She watched in the mirror as she moved one hand down her stomach and over her patch of hair. She could see when she separated her fingers to tease herself. No direct contact was made with her clit, although every nerve in her body felt attuned to that specific body part.

She closed her fingers over her swollen lips, scissoring them before dipping her fingers inside. She sat, mesmerized, as she watched her fingers move in and out of herself, driving deeper with each thrust. Her arousal was tenfold from watching her actions.

Tulley slowly withdrew her fingers and dragged them to the base of her shaft. She briefly rubbed there, increasing her need for release, but the feeling was too exquisite to pass up. When her breathing was ragged and her clit felt like it would surely explode with no help, she stroked up her shaft and finally drew circles around her hardened nerve center with fingers covered in her own juice.

With a mind of their own, her hips rocked as her circles moved inward. No longer circling, her fingers were pressing directly on her clit, rubbing it with as much pressure as it could take. Her left hand pinched her nipple and her right hand continued to rub, urging her clit to grant her relief.

Deep inside her, a dam of energy burst, shooting electric currents outward and flooding her entire body in white heat. She continued to rub as another dam burst and another until she sat there breathless and exhausted and carefully avoiding any more contact on her tender clit.

Tulley quickly shook herself out of her post-orgasmic stupor. It wasn't helping anything for her to sit around masturbating all day. Nor was it helping to pine over a woman who clearly didn't want her.

She turned the shower on as hot as she could stand it and scrubbed her body, doing her best to scrub away her feelings for Sue at the same time. By the time she'd run out of hot water, she'd admitted to herself it was going to be a long time before she was over Sue.

Tulley knew that by mid-afternoon, some of the girls would start returning from their classes. She also knew she didn't want to be there when that happened. She dressed in tan cargo shorts and a navy blue golf shirt, slipped into her Birkenstocks, and headed out the door just after noon.

With nowhere in particular to go, she wandered along Walnut Street toward charming downtown Fenton. At the seven-block mark, she arrived at one of the two main streets dividing the town into east and west. Theodore was a one-way street heading north and Ryan was one-way heading south. The downtown area existed mostly between these two streets and between Cascade to the north and Resaca to the south.

The sidewalks were paved with cobblestones and the storefronts featured wares that varied from books to hemp products to fine art to travel. It was downtown Fenton that Tulley had first fallen in love with as a young teen when her family had stopped on a trip to Oregon. She'd walked through the serene streets where the people seemed to be moving in their own time zone and knew that's where she wanted to go to school.

The scent of incense, Nag Champa to be exact, tickled her nose, and she followed it into a new age metaphysical store. She was amazed at the selection of jewelry, CDs, candles, flags, statues, incense, and books. She wandered through one section of books that covered religions from all areas of the globe. She walked upstairs and found herself next to a section called Sexuality. The title of one book in particular caught her eye, *But I Thought I Was Straight*.

Looking around to make sure no one would see her, she grabbed the book and walked over to a bench in an alcove where she could sit and read in private. The book talked about growing up in a straight environment. The author was from an accepting family and had known some lesbians as a youngster but assumed she was straight because she was sure if she were gay, she'd feel like some sort of a freak.

Tulley lost herself in the tale that was so similar to hers. The author fell in love with her best friend without being able to identify the emotion. They finally got together, which left her confused, since she swore she was straight. Once she accepted it, a whole new world opened to her. She'd felt free, even though she'd never known she felt trapped.

Tulley wondered why she didn't feel free. She supposed it was because the main difference between her story and the author's was that Sue did not reciprocate her feelings. Tulley felt more trapped than ever now that she realized she was a lesbian. She had no one to talk to, and the woman she wanted wasn't interested. Maybe she should write a book about the frustrations she was feeling to show the other side of the story.

After a time, she put the book back on the shelf and exited the store. She took a deep breath of the clean, warm air and exhaled slowly. Hands in pockets, she continued down Theodore looking in windows and enjoying the afternoon.

She crossed Theodore at Canal Street, two blocks before Resaca and the beginning of the university's campus and continued to Ryan, where she turned north and absently meandered in and out of the stores on that street. She walked into a stationery store without realizing it and had turned to walk back out when a display of journals caught her attention. Tulley had an idea. Since she had no one she felt comfortable enough to talk to about this newest development in her life, she decided to buy one of the shiny, leather-covered books to record her thoughts in.

Still not ready to go back to the house, she continued up to Cascade and followed it to Bremer's Park. There she sat at a picnic table, opened her new best friend, and let the words pour forth.

❖

Sue was filled with mixed emotions as she let herself into the house. For one thing, she was thankful her long day was over. After Tulley had gone to bed, Sue had a horrible time focusing on her report and hadn't completed it until shortly after midnight. Even after she went to bed, she couldn't turn off her mind. She kept replaying the confused look in Tulley's eyes. Then there was the kiss. Sue's breath caught every time she relived the touch of those soft lips on hers. And she relived it over and over. Finally, there was the tequila. Had Tulley been sober, how far would Sue have let it go? Those were the things that kept her up until after two, which made her an exhausted wreck all day.

Her report had been well received, but the praise meant little. She could focus on next to nothing. She kept thinking of Tulley. She knew what she wanted from her. But did Tulley understand? Was Tulley ready? Should Sue allow herself to throw caution to the wind and indulge?

She placed her purse on her bed and followed the sound of voices to the front room where several residents were watching television. Tulley was not among them. She couldn't decide if she was disappointed or not. She made her way to the game room to see if Tulley and her gang were there. Livie and Kelly were, but there was no sign of Tulley. Relieved and frustrated, she went back to her room to contemplate what to do next.

With her libido on high, Sue thought long and hard about what to do with her Friday night. The obvious solution would be to go to the Top Cat and see if Mel or Jo was there. They would be able to take her mind off Tulley. Of that, she had no doubt. But part of her didn't want to forget about her.

Needing to clear her head and release some energy, Sue put on running shorts and a T-shirt and laced her running shoes. She walked the two blocks to the park entrance where she stretched her legs and pondered which path to take. She chose a five-mile loop and started at a nice pace.

❖

Tulley sat at the picnic table in the evening sun and stared at the words that had poured out all afternoon. She was amazed at the depth of her emotions. It wasn't until she had started writing that everything had become clear. She read over what she had written so far.

I don't know what's going on. I've never kissed a woman before, but something, maybe the tequila, made me kiss Sue last night. I realize now I have wanted to kiss her for so long. I've been attracted to her the way I guess other girls are to guys.

She has the most incredible green eyes. They're this really dark color and they feel kind of warm and cold at the same time. But the way she looked at me last night, all I saw was hot. Or maybe I imagined that. I don't know now. I didn't feel so drunk anymore. And we were talking and she was being so nice. And when I told her maybe I didn't like guys, the look in her eyes changed. That's when

I knew she wanted me. She pulled it together fast, but not before she gave that away.

I felt weird then. My stomach did a somersault, and I could feel my pulse race. She wanted me. Whether she'd played with my emotions by acting as a friend didn't matter. All that mattered was she wanted me and she was sitting mere inches from me. I didn't think; I just acted. And she responded. She wanted more. I could feel it in the way she was gripping my head and the way her tongue was all over mine.

And then she quit. And I don't know why she did. I guess she didn't want me. Which sucks. Because I've replayed that kiss over and over. But in my mind it goes further. Much further. And thinking like that is only making me more nuts.

I keep thinking I should have grabbed her and pulled her on top of me on the couch. See why I'm going crazy? I imagine kissing her like that. And then I think she could take my hands and put them where she wanted them. Let's face it; I've never given sex a whole lot of thought. I mean, sure, I've wondered. But with Sue, I have no idea what I wanted to do, I just know I wanted to do it. I was feeling things I didn't understand, but I liked them.

In my mind, she puts my hands on her chest. Whenever I think that, my heart goes a million miles an hour and my crotch clenches. So I just keep imagining it. Who knows what I would have done if she'd let me? But she didn't. She stopped.

Sue slowed her pace as she came out of the tree-lined jogging path and into the picnic area. She was staring into space, not focusing on what she saw when a familiar figure caught her eye. She stopped jogging and walked over to the table where Tulley sat.

"What are you doing here?" She watched as Tulley jumped and quickly closed a book she'd been writing in. "What's that? A homework assignment? On a Friday night?"

"Yeah. I wanted to get a head start on it."

"Why not work at the house?" Sue sat across from her.

"I wasn't in the mood."

"I don't suppose you're uncomfortable there today?"

Tulley felt the heat rising up her neck, coloring her face a deep crimson.

"I think we should talk about it." Sue laid her hand over Tulley's.

Sue watched myriad emotions play across Tulley's face, then, since she hadn't objected, Sue pressed on. "You surprised me last night," she said simply.

"I surprised me."

"Do you understand why I had to stop?"

Tulley stared blankly at her. "Because you don't want me."

"Not even close, Tulley. I do want you." She released Tulley's hand and wiped her palms on her shorts. "Imagine if someone would have walked in. It would have looked like I was taking advantage of a drunk resident. I could have lost my job and you would have been outed. Plus, as much as I'd like to get to know you that way, I want you to be sure it's what you want, too."

Sue stood. "When you've figured out who you are, we can revisit this, okay? But don't think for a second that I don't want you. I'll see you back at the house."

Tulley sat there watching Sue walk off. Her stomach was a mass of butterflies. She mentally kicked herself for not being able to say anything intelligible while she'd had the chance. Sue would have listened to her. She believed it. Instead, she'd sat there like some tongue-tied kid. She didn't need time to figure out who she was. She knew what she wanted and she wanted Sue. She grabbed her journal and stood, taking a deep breath as she steeled herself for the conversation she would have when she got to the house.

The sorority house was quiet when Tulley walked in. Dinner was long over and she assumed most of her sisters had gone out to celebrate the weekend. Tulley was imagining a very private celebration that would happen after she spilled her guts to Sue.

She walked down the hall to Sue's room and stopped in the doorway when she saw Sue sitting at her desk putting makeup on. Tulley's mind went back to the last time she'd seen Sue getting all dolled up. Had that really only been a few days before? It seemed a lifetime ago.

Her blood boiled and nausea kept her from speaking. White-hot jealousy flooded her. Before she could turn away, Sue saw her in the mirror and flashed her a friendly smile.

"Hey, kiddo. What are you up to?"

"Nothing. I see you're busy. I'll catch you later." She spun and beelined it to her room before the tears spilled out.

❖

Sue's eyes adjusted to the darkened atmosphere in the Top Cat, and she surveyed the crowd that filled the place. Jo was shooting pool in her usual jeans and muscle shirt. A newer group of butch women were at the other table. Sue wondered if she could get away with fucking one of them. Not likely with Jo there, she decided.

She continued to take stock of the clientele. There were so many women there she knew she'd be able to forget her troubles, at least for a little while.

"You're here by yourself?" someone yelled in her ear.

Sue turned to see Gaby standing next to her. "Yes. I'm alone. Don't tell me you're interested."

"Not even slightly. I was just wondering if Tulley was here."

"Look around. I don't see her. Maybe you will."

"If I do, I'm taking her home. Just so you know."

"Good luck with that." Sue turned away and literally bumped into Mel, whom she hadn't seen in several months. She stumbled back from the impact. Mel caught her and pulled Sue to her.

"Where are you going in such a huff?"

"Just trying to distance myself from someone. Buy me a shot."

"Okay…anyone I need to concern myself with?"

They each drank a shot of Jägermeister before Sue answered.

"No, you don't need to worry about her. She's just after a friend of mine, and she's annoying and irritating."

Mel signaled the bartender for a couple more shots. They downed them before Mel responded.

"Sounds like this 'friend' might be a little more than that."

Sue waved to the bartender. When the next shots were gone, she said, "Nah. I just don't like the woman that's after her."

"So how are you doing, Sue?"

"I'm doing great," Sue lied as she tried to quell the anger that kept building every time she thought of Gaby's nerve. She raised her arm again, but Mel softly laid her hand on it and pulled it down.

"If you're doing great and your friend is nothing more, why are we pounding Jäger like there's no tomorrow?"

Sue turned on her barstool and tried to look as sultry as possible. "I'm in the mood to party. I thought you'd like that."

"Partying is one thing. You seem like you're out to get drunk."

Sue considered what Mel said. She did want to get drunk. So what? She deserved it. She had developed a crush on an untouchable, uninitiated resident at the house she knew had a crush on her, too. She was frustrated at the situation and even more frustrated sexually. She wanted to be with Tulley at that moment, introducing her to the joys of loving a woman. Since that couldn't happen, she was at the bar, drinking with Mel, hoping to at least get lucky with her.

"I'm just out to have fun," she said. "Let's just have one more, okay? And then maybe we can go to your place?"

Sue stood and slipped her arms around Mel's neck. She leaned her body against Mel's and sought her mouth. But Mel pulled away.

"What are you doing?" Sue pouted.

"As much as I've missed you and as bad as I want you, you don't want me. Why don't you figure out what you want and let me know when that's me?"

Sue spun away and stormed to the door. She didn't need Mel. She needed Tulley, and she was tired of being responsible. It still felt early and she was sure she could get some alone time with Tulley.

She was almost out the door when someone grabbed her arm. It was Mel.

"What? You just told me you don't want me. And now you're not going to let me leave?"

"Sweetheart, you don't do shots. You may feel fine, but I'll feel better if I give you a ride home."

"I'm fine to drive. And I'm sure as hell not leaving my car here overnight."

"Then I'm following you. I just want to make sure you get home safely."

Sue acquiesced and admitted to herself she was relieved when she pulled into her parking space. She was more relieved to watch Mel drive off. She wouldn't have put it past Mel to try to get an invite in. Regardless of what she'd said at the bar.

The back door was unlocked, so she knew it was still early. She passed the kitchen and was pleasantly surprised to see Tulley sitting at the table eating a sandwich. Sue couldn't resist joining her.

"You're home early." Tulley said.

"Yeah. I wasn't as into going out as I thought I was."

"You sound like you still managed to have a few."

"I had a couple of shots with a friend." Sue tried to sound casual.

"The pool player?" Tulley asked.

"No. A different friend." She sat there watching Tulley determinedly avoid eye contact. She'd never seen a person so engrossed in a sandwich. She wanted Tulley desperately at that moment and wondered if the sexual tension was too much for her. She decided she didn't want to wait any longer.

"I don't suppose you'd be willing to come into my room and talk for a bit?"

Tulley's stomach knotted. Who knew who Sue had already been with that night? She was more jealous than she'd ever been. Would she be able to play it cool and just hang out and talk with her? She found she couldn't pass on the opportunity to spend time with Sue in any capacity.

"Sure. We could do that."

Sue closed the door behind them and motioned for Tulley to join her on the bed.

Tulley sat with her back against the wall and tried to keep her thoughts clean as Sue lay back with her head on the pillow. She needn't have worried.

Sue took her hand and pulled Tulley to her. She ran her fingers through Tulley's hair as she claimed her mouth with her own. Tulley quickly responded to the kiss, and soon found herself on top of Sue.

Tulley could barely breathe. Everything was perfect. Sue was under her, each curve pressing into her, filling her with desire. No, not everything was perfect. Her breath tasted like Jägermeister. It seemed strong enough to get her drunk, too.

She abruptly stopped kissing Sue and slid off her.

"What are you doing?" Sue croaked. "You can't start something like this and then put the brakes on. It's not fair."

"I'm not one of them." Tulley stood on shaky legs.

"*Them?*"

"The women at the bar that you can use whenever you're in the mood. I know you think I'm confused, but let me just say that I know what I want. And that's you. When you figure out it's me you want and not just some warm body in your bed, get back to me, okay? Good night, Sue."

Tulley stormed out of the room and slammed the door behind her. Her heart was pounding, and she hoped to God she'd done the right thing and not blown the only chance she might ever get to be with the woman of her dreams.

Chapter Eleven

Tulley stood with a bowl of cereal in her hand while she waited for the congestion in the kitchen to clear. The refrigerator seemed like a distant island surrounded by a sea of people. She wasn't in the mood to deal with anyone, but her roommates had allowed them to run out of milk. Plus the inane chatter around her was annoying, which didn't help nerves already on edge for fear of seeing Sue.

"Do you have a second?" She heard the soft voice in her ear. "We should talk."

Tulley started and stepped away. "Now's not good. I've got stuff to work on as soon as I finish breakfast."

"Don't be that way, Tulley."

She looked around and realized the gazes of the other women in the kitchen were trained on them. "How about I work for a couple of hours and then meet with you?"

"Okay. You can come get me when you have time."

"Oh, my. Did I miss a lovers' quarrel?" Danielle asked from the doorway that led to the dining room.

Tulley turned to face her, ignoring the other women behind her. "Shut the fuck up, Danielle. Just once, mind your own fucking business."

But Danielle was not to be discouraged. "Touchy, touchy."

"Yeah, I'm touchy. I'm so fucking tired of your bullshit. You make shit up in that empty head and spew your fucked up ideas where they're not welcome. So just shut up. Jesus Christ."

She slammed her bowl down and left the room, too pissed to care that nearly fifteen people, including Sue, stared at her, wondering what had finally set her off.

❖

"Do you think that little scene helped anything?" Sue let herself into Tulley's room.

"Yeah, as a matter of fact. It helped me feel better. How about if I screw the rest of you and just think about me once in a while?"

"Let's get out of here. Let's get away from the house and just go somewhere to talk."

"Talk? What is there to say?" Tulley asked.

Sue looked around nervously. "We have plenty to say. We just can't say anything here. Get dressed and meet me at my car in ten minutes."

Tulley rolled over and tried to give serious thought to not going with Sue. She felt like a worthless puppy that would come whenever Sue snapped her fingers. She wished she understood her emotions. Being with Sue made her happier than she'd ever been. And being with Sue inflicted an ungodly amount of pain and frustration. She knew in her heart of hearts she should stay where she was and forget about Sue.

But there was no way she was going to say no to Sue and she knew it. She slipped into a pair of cotton shorts and pulled a Fenton State T-shirt over her wifebeater. A few of her sisters were in the bathroom when she got there to brush her teeth, but they just gave her a strange look and moved away. Tulley was fine with that. When she was through, she hurried downstairs and out the back door without a word to anyone. Certain no one noticed her, she let herself in Sue's car and waited.

Her heart was pounding as scenario after scenario played through her head. She imagined climbing into the tiny backseat with Sue and touching her all over, kissing her the way they kissed the night before. She felt like she was going to have a heart attack when the driver's door opened.

"Where are we going?" Tulley tried to sound cool.

"I thought we'd drive through the park. It's supposed to be hot today, and I thought it would be nice to go sit by the creek at the upper end and relax."

Tulley couldn't even imagine relaxing while spending a day with Sue, but she'd do anything Sue wanted, so she didn't argue.

Sue drove through the lower portion of the park, quietly thinking of everything she wanted to do with Tulley. She knew she'd have to take it slow, and she vowed to try. But she also knew she couldn't promise anything once she got Tulley away from people in the privacy of Upper Park.

The silence in the car became awkward, so Sue took a deep breath. "I'm sorry about last night."

"So am I. I said some harsh things. I didn't mean them."

"I deserved them, I suppose."

Tulley looked over at her with an arched eyebrow.

"I mean, I can see why you'd think that of me. But you're different."

"How? Why? And why tell me that? Why not just let me get over you? I feel like some little kid with a crush. Why don't you just accept it as cute and send me on my way?"

"Because I don't want you heading on your way. I want to see where this goes."

"What chance do we have? We're doomed from the beginning. Look where we live. And it's not just that it's a sorority house. Like you said, you're an authority figure. How's that gonna fly?"

"How about you and I figure things out before we worry about explaining things to anyone else?" Sue parked her car on the dirt plateau overlooking the creek.

"Fair enough."

"Now come on. We're going to relax and enjoy the day. Do you see those flat rocks down there?" She pointed to a nature-made bed just yards up from the water.

"Sure."

"That's where we'll be for the next few hours. Follow me. The trail's a little tricky."

Sue swayed her hips for Tulley's pleasure as she led the way. She smiled to herself, imagining Tulley trying to focus on her footing and not be mesmerized by her ass. They safely reached the rocks and Tulley lay back, basking in the midday sun.

Sue stood over her, blocking the sun.

"What are you doing?" Tulley laughed.

"Last one in is a rotten egg." Sue immediately stripped and jumped into the cold creek rushing by.

Tulley couldn't move. Every muscle in her body, including those she'd never paid much attention to, was contracted with sheer need as she saw every perfect inch of Sue's naked body before it disappeared under water.

She sat up and watched Sue tread water, amazed that she was actually in the cold water.

"Come on, chicken!" Sue called.

"Are you crazy?"

"Maybe. But get in here."

Tulley wasn't about to be shown up, so she stood and took her shirt off. "Hey, you can't watch me."

"Why?"

Tulley knew she was bright red. She was also more aroused than she'd ever been. Something about Sue watching her strip turned her on in a way she didn't even know was possible. Still, she knew she'd never be able to do it. She didn't have it in her.

"Fine. Be that way." Sue turned and faced the other shore.

Not fully trusting her to stay like that, Tulley stripped quickly and let out a slight scream as she jumped in next to Sue.

"This water's freakin' freezing!" she yelled when she surfaced.

"Move around then. Swim. That'll keep you warm."

Tulley started to swim in the other direction but felt Sue's hand close on her ankle and pull her back.

"You're not helping."

Sue moved so her body was against Tulley's even as her legs moved rhythmically, keeping her afloat. Tulley made no move to pull away.

"Are you a strong swimmer?" Sue asked.

"Very. Why?"

Sue wrapped her arms around Tulley's neck and her legs around her waist and kissed her hard on her mouth. She felt Tulley's immediate surprise but then felt the young muscles working at keeping them both above water.

Tulley's kisses were far more confident than their first night's. There was no hesitation in anything she did. She held Sue close, and Sue reveled in the feel of her body. Tulley moved her hands lower as she cupped Sue's ass, pulling her mons against her.

Sue broke the kiss first. She brushed Tulley's hair out of her eyes and stared into them.

"You doing okay?"

"Never better."

"You sure?"

If it was proof Sue wanted, Tulley was more than happy to give it to her. Kissing her again, her own mouth devouring Sue's, she managed to direct them toward the shore. They held hands as they raced for their flat rocks and the chance to test the waters of their new relationship.

Sue lay down and pulled Tulley on top of her. As they continued to kiss, Sue shifted slightly so Tulley's knee was between her legs. Tulley felt Sue's heat radiating on her and her breath caught.

The feel of Sue's bare skin under hers was more than Tulley had ever dreamed of. She felt connected to her on so many levels. It was more than just sex. She knew that. There was something so much deeper, and Tulley had fallen all the way in. She was still not sure what was to come, but she knew she couldn't stand the thought of not feeling everything she felt right then.

Her heart was thudding in her chest. She felt sure it would explode. She was full of so many emotions and sensations.

"Whatcha thinking?" Sue asked.

Tulley thought that was the most ridiculous question she'd ever heard. "Why would you ask me that?"

"I'm just curious." Sue dragged her fingernails along Tulley's back and smiled as her nipples puckered tighter. "You like that, huh?"

"I really like you, Sue."

"I know, Tulley. And I really like you."

Sue watched Tulley's eyes as she slowly moved herself to her knee.

Tulley's breath caught and her eyes shut as she felt the slick heat of Sue against her. Instinct took over and she moved her knee against Sue while she lowered her mouth to one of Sue's extended nipples.

Sue grasped Tulley's head with both hands and arched her back, encouraging Tulley to take more, suck harder. She moved against her leg with wanton abandon, rubbing fast and hard. Tulley continued to press into her, forcing herself to keep time with the rhythm Sue had set.

Tulley could feel Sue's body tensing up, and she tried to focus on everything at once, but the sensations were overwhelming. She was aware of Sue in an ethereal way, even as she felt her moving against and under her. She was lost in the dizziness she was feeling when Sue moved her mouth back to hers and kissed her while she pulled Tulley against her. Sue's whole body tensed as she whimpered, moving up and down frantically on Tulley's leg.

Confused, Tulley hoped she was doing her part as she let Sue's orgasm wash over her.

Tulley watched as Sue struggled to catch her breath, and was relieved when she said, "Oh, my God, that was amazing. I've wanted you for so long. I've fantasized about your touch for months now. I'm sorry I was so selfish, but I needed that."

"So that was good then, huh?" Tulley was trying to wrap her mind around what had just happened. She knew it felt right and left no doubt in her mind that she was truly a lesbian. But there was more to it than that. There was a sense of awe that she had helped Sue to an orgasm. The wonder of it mingled with the pride she felt. Any confusion at all vanished as she lay looking at Sue. She felt an overwhelming sense of relief at finally knowing who she was. And she embraced it with every ounce of her being.

"What do you think?"

"I think it was amazing. It's kind of mind-blowing actually."

"How so?"

"I don't know how else to put it, but it was totally awesome to be able to give you an orgasm." Tulley didn't know exactly how to say what a pleasure and honor it had been to make Sue come. She felt foolish as she thought of the indescribable beauty of Sue's face as the orgasm coursed through her. She knew she wanted to see it again, though.

Sue laughed and rolled over so Tulley was on her back. She took one of Tulley's nipples in her mouth as her hand moved lower and traced lines from the top of her curls to her belly button and back again.

"How you doing now?"

"You make me feel so much. Inside and out. Do I sound like an idiot?"

"Not at all. I want to make you feel good, Tull. But you need to tell me if anything doesn't feel right."

"You're scaring me."

"Don't be scared, sweetheart. Just relax."

As she spoke, Sue let her fingers dip lower and lower until they were in Tulley's wet curls. She circled Tulley's swollen clit and heard her sharp intake of breath. She slid her fingers lower and dipped the tip of one finger inside Tulley.

She propped herself so she could watch Tulley's face and her own hand. She slipped her finger all the way in and heard Tulley gasp.

"So no one has ever touched you like this before?"

"No."

"Thank you for letting me."

She moved her finger in and out before slipping another one into the growing wetness between Tulley's legs.

Tulley began writhing on the rock. Sue was pleasing her and frustrating her, making her feel things she'd never known possible. She was feeling too good. Something had to give, but she didn't know what. She had to do something but was too overwhelmed to think what that something might be. In all the times she'd touched herself, she knew what to do next, but now there were too many sensations at once. She was so close to coming but was almost too overwhelmed to let go.

"Relax," Sue said, pressing into Tulley's walls as she slowly removed her fingers. She started rubbing Tulley just above her clit and continued rubbing little circles as she moved lower and lower. Tulley was throbbing at Sue's touch. Sue stroked the tender underside and was rewarded when Tulley screamed out at the top of her lungs.

"Oh, my God," Tulley said much more calmly when the spasms had settled down. "Oh, my God. No wonder people have sex."

Sue laughed loudly. "You're such a romantic."

"I'm sorry. It's just that—"

"Shh. Don't worry. I understand exactly what you were saying." Sue kissed Tulley softly.

Tulley wanted to please Sue the way she had pleasured her. She wanted more than just to have Sue rub her leg. She wanted to savor Sue's beautiful, supple body.

She ended the kiss and bent to take one of Sue's long, hard nipples in her mouth. She was rewarded when she heard a long moan from Sue. She licked and sucked for what seemed an eternity. She couldn't get enough of her breasts. She kneaded first one and then the other as she took turns sucking and nibbling. She could have stayed there forever, but she felt Sue pressing on the top of her head, urging her downward.

Unsure of what to do but knowing she had to try, Tulley trailed kisses down Sue's taut belly.

"Please, baby, press your tits into my pussy. I love how that feels."

Tulley did as she was instructed and was pleasantly surprised at how good Sue's slick juices felt all over her breasts. She moved lower and replaced her breasts with her tongue, tasting Sue for the first time.

She was immediately dizzy from the heady flavor. She licked Sue from pussy to clit and back again, determined to devour every drop of juice. Yet the more she licked, the more juice there was. She tried to think what Sue would like and immediately went to work licking and sucking her clit. Soon, all thinking was gone as she simply did what felt best, then followed the signals Sue gave her through her movements. It seemed to take no time at all before Sue pressed her head, holding her mouth in place as her tongue flicked her clit.

Sue arched her back to greet Tulley's tongue, then froze as she screamed in pleasure as the orgasm washed over her.

Tulley was content to lick her clean, but Sue finally pulled her to her and kissed her hard.

"So where does this leave us?" Tulley asked, hopeful yet terrified.

"This means you're mine."

"Which means you're mine. No one else's," Tulley said pointedly.

"I am." Sue snuggled close to Tulley, who wrapped an arm around her and held her tight as they fell asleep in the afternoon sun.

❖

Sue parked the car a few blocks from the house so they could get one more brief make out session before they got home after a day of sleeping, swimming, and making love.

"It's gonna suck being back," Tulley said as they came up for air.

"In a big way. Just remember to be careful. We can't let anyone find out."

"I know. So when I want to grab you and kiss you, I'll just walk away. Just in case you wonder why I walk off mid-conversation."

"Somehow I don't think that will be smooth." Sue laughed.

"You know what's smooth?" Tulley ran her hand up Sue's thigh as she kissed her again.

Sue lay back and spread her legs as best as her little car would allow as Tulley's fingers played along the length of her. Tulley sucked and nibbled her neck while she teased beneath those short pink shorts.

"I need you in me," Sue whispered. "Please."

Tulley obliged and pounded deep inside Sue until Sue felt her pussy tighten around Tulley's fingers, holding them in place while she rode the two orgasms Tulley had provided.

When Sue's pussy finally released Tulley's fingers, they kissed a little longer until Sue said they needed to get home.

"Why? Can't we just pretend we both happened to be gone for the weekend? Can't we go somewhere?"

"Oh, my dear, sweet Tulley. If only it were that easy. For me to go away, I'd have to have registered with the house committee. Since I didn't, I'm pretty much required to be there."

"I still don't get why you live under such tight restrictions. I don't think I could handle your job."

"Speaking of my job, I need to get back to it. Buckle up."

They walked in the back door, and Tulley's gut wrenched at the thought of having to leave Sue to go up to her own room. Before she could say anything, Danielle walked out of the kitchen.

"I smell sex," she said.

"Well, if anyone would know what that smelled like…" Tulley said.

Sue came out of her room as the crowd in the kitchen quieted. "That's enough, ladies. I wish you two would try to get along."

Danielle looked first at Tulley, then at Sue. "My, my. Don't we both have wicked sunburns? I'm curious, do either of you have tan lines? My bet is no."

Tulley heard the murmurs come from the kitchen as Danielle arched a perfectly shaped eyebrow at her and walked away.

Sue stood there, looking unsure of herself

Tulley spoke first, in a low tone. "She doesn't know anything for sure. We're safe."

"I know." Sue said. "For now, let's just avoid each other to alleviate any more talk."

"What? I don't know if I can do that."

"For now, we have to. Please. For me."

"Okay. But not for too long, promise?"

"I promise."

Sue was unable to follow her own advice, and shortly before noon the next day, she was wandering from room to room looking for Tulley. She found her shooting pool by herself in the game room.

She stood back and admired the tight ass on Tulley as she bent over for a shot. She longed to run her hand up a thigh and press into the wetness she knew was waiting. Sue knew she shouldn't be there, but she couldn't help herself. The draw to Tulley was intoxicating, like a drug. She just hoped it wasn't as dangerous.

Tulley finished her shot and turned to see Sue staring at her.

"What happened to staying away from each other?"

"I can't do it. I need to be alone with you."

"Does that mean you need to—"

"It means I need to be alone with you, wise ass."

Tulley grinned. "And just how do you propose we pull this off?"

"I'll pack us a picnic."

"Oh, good. No one will be suspicious then."

"Would you let me finish?"

"Go ahead." Tulley leaned back against the table.

"I will be careful. I'll pack us a picnic and drive over to Bremer's Park. You walk over and get in the car and we'll drive back up to the upper area again."

"You're sneaky," Tulley said appreciatively. "What time does 'Operation Rendezvous' take place?"

"Listen to you. Just be there in an hour, okay?"

"God, I want to kiss you," Tulley whispered.

Sue looked around, terrified that someone might have heard. "You can't say that. Even if we think there's no one around. But I will say hold that thought for an hour. I'll see you then."

The pickup at the park went off without a hitch, and soon they were at the same place as the day before. They quickly peeled the clothes off each other and lay on the hot rock, hands roaming all over their bodies.

They kissed, they touched, they loved each other under the sun with only Mother Nature in on their secret. Hours passed before they lay temporarily satiated in each other's arms.

"I don't know about you, but I'm starving." Sue sat up and reached for the beach bag she brought.

She handed Tulley a sandwich and a Pepsi, then grabbed one each for herself. They enjoyed the silence of their togetherness while they ate until Sue spoke.

"You know, Tulley, I've been giving a lot of thought to what you said last night."

"What part?"

"About my job. I don't mind it and I think we could pull it off, not easily, but I think we could do it if it weren't for Danielle and her ilk."

"I wish I knew what her problem is. And why does she have to announce everything to the house? Why can't she just give us shit? You'd think that would be enough for her."

"I agree. She's got some issues that aren't for us to figure out. The point is, I really want to give this a chance, but we need to be careful around the house. I can't afford to lose my position there."

"So what will we do?" Tulley rolled Sue over to her back.

"I think we'll just have to figure out a way to get away for a weekend or two."

"I like the sound of that."

"There are motels in town we can go to."

"Oh yeah. A weekend in a room with you? That sounds like Heaven."

She kissed Sue slowly, languidly, lovingly. Their tongues rolled over each other like they were lovers with nothing but time. Tulley kissed away from Sue's mouth, down her neck to where her shoulder and neck came together. She sucked there and lightly bit her, smiling at the effect she had on Sue.

Tulley continued to kiss down Sue's chest until she reached her erect nipples and sucked and licked first one then the other before kissing her way to Sue's taut belly.

As she trailed her kisses from Sue's belly button down, Tulley pressed her breasts into Sue's waiting pussy.

"God, I love that feeling," Sue gasped.

"As do I."

Soon Sue was writhing on the rock.

"I can't take much more teasing, sweetheart," Sue said.

Tulley kissed over Sue's smooth mons and lowered her shoulders so Sue could place her legs over them. With unimpeded access, Tulley licked the length of Sue from the satin walls of her pussy, between her swollen wet lips, along the underside, and around the head of her turgid clit.

She focused on Sue's clit, licking around it, across it, even sucking it between her teeth while her tongue teased the tender underside. When Sue was close, Tulley moved lower and licked the slick walls of Sue's pussy, running her tongue deep inside and evoking sensations that made Sue shudder.

As Sue began to whimper, Tulley flattened her tongue and lapped at the whole area between Sue's legs. Over and over with more and more pressure, she pressed into every inch of her. Sue arched her hips to meet every lick and was rewarded with Tulley's tongue directly on her clit. Again and again, her tongue assailed the engorged clit until Sue's cries echoed down the waterway as the waves of her orgasms cascaded over her.

When she came back to Earth and Tulley lay holding her, Sue said, "As much as I love making love out here, I'm looking forward to some time in a bed with you sometime."

"Sometime soon, I hope," Tulley said.

"Sometime soon," Sue agreed.

CHAPTER TWELVE

Tulley sat at the table with Gaby trying to focus on their women's studies project, but her mind was a million miles away. They had gotten together at four o'clock, and by the time it was past five, Tulley was almost useless. She knew Sue would be arriving home any time, and she wanted to get home to see her.

"What's with you?" Gaby finally asked.

"What do you mean?"

"You've got the attention span of a gnat today. We need to get this done. You're not having second thoughts about our project, are you?"

Tulley was silent while she thought how best to answer the question. It wasn't the project she was having second thoughts about. She just didn't enjoy being around Gaby.

"I'm fine. It's just Monday, you know. Who's up for a project on Monday?" She tried to joke.

"Well, you seem a little distracted today. As long as you say you're okay."

The last thing Tulley planned on doing was telling Gaby about Sue. She was fairly certain Gaby's feelings weren't platonic, and she didn't want to hurt her or encourage her to step up her game.

"I almost forgot." Gaby reached into her hemp messenger bag. "I saw something this weekend and had to get it for you."

She handed a box to Tulley, who took it with trepidation.

"Go ahead. It won't bite." Gaby laughed.

Tulley opened the box, and there was a statue of two naked cherubs—one reclining on a leaf and the other feeding it grapes.

"It's nothing big," Gaby said. "Like I said, I saw it and thought of you."

Tulley stared at the artwork and thought she'd never been so uncomfortable. She didn't consider Gaby thinking of her when she saw two tiny naked babies was such a good thing.

"You know, because your folks have a vineyard and all."

"It's cute. Really. Thank you." Tulley couldn't imagine where Gaby might have been that she just happened to run into an artifact like that. "Where did you find it?"

Gaby said nothing for a moment and then answered, "I picked it up at Saturday Market. There are all kinds of artisans there. You never know what you'll find."

At that point, Tulley strongly felt the need to get home to Sue. She didn't want to spend another minute around Gaby. But Gaby seemed to have other ideas.

"I saw your friend at the bar the other night," Gaby said.

Tulley had to stop and think. The past two days had seemed like an eternity with everything going on in her life. When had Sue been at the bar?

"It was Friday night," she continued. "She was downing shots with some dark-haired buff woman."

Tulley had to fight the jealousy boiling up inside her. She reminded herself that was the night she had walked away from Sue. She knew she'd been at the bar. Her life with Sue officially began the next day. She had no reason to be angry.

"She didn't mention seeing you," Tulley said, trying to play it cool. "Did you have a good time?"

"I did, but not as much fun as it looked like your friend was having."

Tulley felt her head about to explode. All she wanted was for Gaby to shut up about it.

"Yeah. She said she had a good time Friday. She didn't stay late but still had fun."

It seemed to work. Gaby didn't say another word about it.

"You know what? You're right. I can't get into studying today. I'm going to bail."

Gaby looked panicked. "Was it something I said? Please. Stay here for a while. We need to get more done on this."

"No, we don't. We've got over two months until it's due. I'll work with you Wednesday, but for now, I'm just not feeling it. Sorry."

Tulley stood to leave, but Gaby didn't give up.

"Why don't we go out to the Top Cat? Have a couple of beers? My treat. I feel like we haven't connected in too long."

Tulley bit her tongue. She refrained from pointing out they had only met the previous week.

"No, thanks. I've got work to do in other classes. I'm just going to go home and work on that. I really am sorry to blow off studying, but I promise we'll get together Wednesday."

She scurried away from the table and out of the library, taking in a deep breath of the fresh air of freedom. Tulley had felt so trapped with Gaby, and the air had begun to feel stagnant. The evening air outside was comfortably in the eighties, and she smiled to herself as she enjoyed her walk up the few blocks to the sorority house.

Tulley let herself in the back door and didn't realize she'd been holding her breath until she saw Sue lounging on her bed, reading. She stopped in the doorway, unsure that she'd be able to control herself if she got too close.

"Hey, Tulley," Sue said normally, but her eyes conveyed emotions and desires Tulley wished they could act on. "How was your day?"

"Long."

The look Sue gave her told her she understood exactly why. "I hear that."

"It was worse than your normal Monday."

"Yeah, mine was, too."

"Oh, yeah, Gaby gave me a gift tonight."

"She did? Come in and show it to me."

Tulley got the box out of her backpack and handed it to Sue, who closed her fingers over Tulley's during the hand off.

"This is interesting. Does she think this is you and her?"

"Very funny."

"Did you tell her? About the weekend?"

"No, but it was tempting, the way she kept going on and on about seeing you at the bar Friday night."

"I'm sorry, Tull."

"It's okay. Someday I'll get to tell her." Tulley didn't want to leave, but standing there unable to jump Sue was unbearable. "I'm going to go up to my room until dinner. I guess I'll see you then."

"I guess you will."

Dinner that night was torture for Tulley. She did her best not to make eye contact with Sue for fear her feelings would show. Yet she felt that it was obvious to everyone that she was avoiding her. More than once, she stared at her plate, her mind flashing back to the weekend and the hours of enjoyment she'd found in Sue's arms.

She was sure the rest of the house could feel the tension and forced herself not to respond when Danielle mouthed off.

"Is it just me, or is there some awkward silence here tonight?"

"I hadn't noticed," Sue said.

"Really? Because you seem uncomfortable." She shrugged. "Not that it matters to me or anything. I just wondered if anyone wanted to tell the rest of us what's going on?"

Tulley focused on her food even as she felt Danielle's gaze land on her. She hated Danielle and resented her for making her situation with Sue more complicated than it had to be.

A few of the others pushed their chairs back and carried their plates to the kitchen. Silence fell again.

"It's not good to keep secrets," Danielle said. "They tend to fester and backfire on you."

Tulley breathed a sigh of relief as Danielle left the table. She waited until she saw Danielle leave the kitchen before she, too, stepped away from the table to rinse her plate.

When she got to her room, Kelly and Livie were sitting on Livie's bed. Tulley lay on hers. The two others said nothing, just stared at Tulley.

"What?" Tulley said, annoyed.

"Is something going on?" Livie finally asked.

"I don't know what you're talking about."

"Between you and Sue."

Tulley let out a heavy sigh. "Not you two now."

"Even if you two were an item, you couldn't say anything, could you?" Kelly asked.

"Why does everyone assume there's something between Sue and me?"

"To start with, you two spent an awful lot of time together over the weekend and then wouldn't even look at each other at dinner," Livie pointed out.

"Maybe she had a rough day. I know I did. Does that equate to an affair? And yeah, we hung out over the weekend. We're friends. That's what joining this stupid organization is all about, isn't it? To make friends for life? And stupidly, I thought you guys were my friends, too."

"We are," Kelly said. "We just wondered, so we asked rather than listen to rumors. That's what friends do."

"Okay," Livie said. "You say there's nothing between you. Which could be true. Or you could be protecting Sue. How about you promise to tell Kelly and me if something does develop between you two so we don't have to hear about it from someone else?"

"Whatever. It's not like we're gay anyway, so you two are barking up the wrong tree."

Livie and Kelly looked at each other.

"Sue may not broadcast her sexuality, but she doesn't exactly hide the fact that she's a lesbian. And it would be okay with us if you were, too," Kelly said.

"But I'm not." Tulley did her best to sound exasperated. She wished she could make herself come out to her friends, but she just wasn't ready. Part of it, she knew, was that she didn't want to get Sue in trouble. But there was more. There was fear of the ridicule and harassment from people like Danielle. And she was fully aware that when she told Kelly and Livie, it would only be a matter of time before everyone knew. She didn't delude herself into thinking secrets were kept in a sorority house.

She also knew she wasn't ready to share whatever it was she had with Sue. It was new and exciting and she liked to savor it and keep it between the two of them for now. She tried to tell herself that, but the fear always came back. What if her family found out? There were lesbians working in the vineyard and her parents were fine with them, but how would they feel if it was their daughter? There were too many risks for her to come out yet. Livie's talking brought her back to the moment.

"And if you're not, that's okay, too. But if you are and you're involved, that's okay because we think Sue is a wonderful lady, and we think you two would be awesome together."

Tulley had to roll over and face the wall lest her roommates see the beaming smile on her face.

"That's all we'll say."

"Fine," Tulley said, rolling back over. "Now that we're through in imagination nation, let's go shoot some pool."

Sue and Tulley spent as much time together as they could over the next few weeks. School kept them both busy, but they quickly determined how to use the library for more than simply studying. What started as making out between the shelves soon turned into taking over private study rooms.

"We're never going to get any work done." Tulley laughed the first time she and Sue used a room.

"Sure we will." Sue smiled as she locked the door. "We'll just also have fun."

She moved into Tulley's arms and kissed her. She felt Tulley's hands on her ass, pulling her close.

"I do like fun," Tulley murmured against Sue's mouth.

Sue pried Tulley's lips apart and slid her tongue inside her mouth as she backed up and sat on the table. She wrapped her legs around Tulley as their kiss intensified. Tulley moved her mouth away and kissed down Sue's cheek and neck while her hand slid under Sue's blouse. She closed her fingers around Sue's nipple and Sue bit her lip to keep from crying out.

Tulley got Sue's shirt up and bent to kiss an exposed breast.

"Oh fuck, Tulley. You're making me crazy." Sue was very happy with the progress Tulley had made as a lover. She had quickly learned what Sue liked and seemed to take great pleasure in taking care of her.

Tulley moved her hand lower and unbuttoned Sue's shorts.

"You're not wasting any time, are you?" Sue asked.

"I need to be in you," Tulley unzipped the shorts and stepped back to peel them off. She sat in a chair and kissed up one of Sue's inner thighs.

"Please don't tease me," Sue begged.

Tulley kissed Sue's clit while she slid her fingers inside.

"Damn, you're wet."

"Fuck me, Tulley. Give me more."

Tulley plunged her fingers in deep, then quickly pulled them out before driving them in again. She flicked Sue's clit with her tongue and Sue placed her hand on the back of Tulley's head to hold her mouth in place.

She arched her hips to take Tulley deeper and encourage her tongue to lap harder.

"Oh, God, baby. Oh yes, you feel so good." She closed her eyes and blocked out everything but the sensations between her legs. It didn't take long until the explosion started at her core and she gave herself over to the orgasm that coursed through her. She closed her legs tightly around Tulley as she rode the crest, then floated back to Earth.

Tulley extricated herself from the death grip Sue's legs had on her and stood. She bent over the table and kissed Sue, slipping her tongue in Sue's mouth. When Tulley finally broke the kiss, Sue was breathless.

"Damn, I taste good," she said.

"Yeah, you do."

Sue sat up and reached for Tulley's shorts.

"Let's get these off of you."

Tulley quickly obliged and was soon standing in front of Sue in just her shirt. Sue took Tulley's shirt off and leaned in to take a nipple in her mouth. She loved feeling the hard nub swell against her tongue. She licked around and over it before closing her lips and sucking.

She heard Tulley gasp as she ran her hand down her belly and between her legs. She found Tulley's pussy slick with need. Sue buried her fingers within her tight walls and pressed her palm into her throbbing clit.

She continued to suck first one, then the other nipple as Tulley swayed in her efforts to remain standing. She finally placed her hands on Sue's shoulders and held on.

Sue smiled to herself as Tulley tried to retain her balance. She withdrew her fingers and ran them over her clit. She felt Tulley lower as her knees buckled. She wrapped her free arm around her and held her.

"Are you close, babe?"

"God, yes."

"I've got you. Just relax and let go."

"Oh fuck, Sue," Tulley moaned as she froze and then collapsed against her. "Oh fuck."

"That was nice." Sue took her fingers from between Tulley's legs and licked them clean.

"Yeah, it was. Holy shit."

"And now we should probably study."

"I'd rather nap," Tulley said.

"You need to keep up with your schoolwork or we're not going to be able to spend this much time together."

"Yeah, yeah, yeah." Tulley moved away and got dressed, after handing Sue's clothes to her. "I get that. I'm just so relaxed right now."

"Well, we need to study for a while. There's no rule that we can't make love again in a while."

Tulley kissed her. "I love the way you think."

CHAPTER THIRTEEN

Sue lay in bed that night, replaying her day with Tulley. She had a smile on her face, as usual. It had become a fairly permanent fixture lately. She was really into Tulley. She made her laugh, she made her think, she got her hot. She was a lot of fun.

There was something else, though, and Sue challenged herself to figure out what it was. Since they'd been seeing each other, Sue hadn't felt the need to seek out Jo or Mel or any of her usual bedmates. She toyed with the idea of setting something up the following night, but if she was honest with herself, she had no desire to see any of them. She was smitten with Tulley. She didn't understand it, but there was no denying it.

She couldn't get enough of her. In between classes, Sue kept her eyes peeled in case she might catch a glimpse of her crossing campus. When she was at the house, her ears were constantly on alert for the sound of Tulley's voice. Every evening, she looked forward to dinner at the house with equal parts anticipation and dread. She enjoyed being in the same room with Tulley, enjoying an everyday thing like a meal, but she also hated the charade that they were nothing more than friends.

The smile on Sue's face faded slightly. If she was completely honest with herself, Tulley reminded her a lot of Tabitha. They both had that same adorable shyness with a desire to break out of their shells. Tabitha had always been content to stay in the background, letting Sue be the wild one. Although, like Tulley, it wasn't possible for Tabitha to go unnoticed. Men and women wanted her. Sue had counted her blessings that Tabitha had chosen her.

Sue sat up and leaned against the wall. Her stomach knotted as she continued to play out her time with Tabitha. The major difference between Tabitha and Tulley was that Tabitha had seemed comfortable being a lesbian even as a freshman. She didn't want to be out or anything, but she seemed so secure in her sexuality when they were together.

That was the main reason it hurt so much when she'd said she was through playing and ready to move on with real life. Sue had been blindsided. She'd seen Tabitha as someone she'd be with forever.

She pondered whether Tulley might simply be testing the waters, but soon disregarded the thought. Sure, she was young and just coming out, but Sue was fairly confident she needn't fear Tulley waking up straight one day.

She settled back under the covers and replayed her day again as she drifted off to sleep.

"Remember where to go after school tomorrow night," Sue reminded Tulley on Thursday night as they sat talking in Sue's room.

"How could I forget? I'll beeline it to the hotel as soon as I can after my last class."

"I'll have us all checked in so you can go straight to our room."

"No worries. I'm not about to forget." She rose from Sue's bed. "And now, I need to get out of here before I do something to get us both in trouble. I'm going to bed. I'll see you tomorrow."

❖

The next day seemed to last forever for Tulley. She spent much of it staring at the clocks on the walls of her classrooms, wishing them to speed up. By the time she got to her three-hour women's studies class at two, she wondered why she'd even bothered going to school. Nothing was sinking in. Her mind was already with Sue at the hotel.

Sue had come up with the excellent idea of making up excuses why they each had to be out of town that weekend. Then she rented a room in a hotel just off campus. With no one expecting them at the house, they could spend the whole weekend together in a hotel room, needing nothing but each other. Tulley was so ready for the weekend to begin.

As soon as class was over, Tulley crammed her books into her backpack, but before she could stand, Gaby was at her desk.

"Hey there, what do you say we go shoot some pool or something tonight?"

"I'd love to, but I've made other plans."

"Really? Like what?"

Tulley stared at her, unable to believe her nerve.

"I'm meeting a friend to study."

"Are we ever gonna hang out again? I feel like you're avoiding me."

"I'm not avoiding you," Tulley lied. "I just have a lot going on."

"Well, when your busy social calendar has an opening, let me know." Gaby stormed out.

Tulley sat there wondering if Gaby treated all the women she liked like that. She didn't see it as a way to winning hearts and wooing women. But that wasn't her concern. She grabbed her backpack and cut across campus to meet with Sue.

The door was locked and the curtains were closed when Tulley arrived. She knocked on the door, and when it opened, there stood Sue in a black baby doll negligee.

"Come on in."

"Holy shit. You look amazing."

Sue grabbed Tulley's arm and pulled her into the room, closing and locking the door behind her. She pressed Tulley against the door and snaked her arms around her neck.

"Welcome home," she whispered just before kissing her with all the passion they'd been nurturing over the past couple of weeks. She broke the kiss and took Tulley by the hand, leading her into the master bedroom, where the mattress lay covered with rose petals.

Tulley took Sue in her arms and kissed her hard on her mouth while she slowly and carefully laid them both on the mattress. She continued kissing, her tongue dancing passionately with Sue's as she slid her hand under the top of the negligee and lightly ran it over Sue's soft belly.

Sue gently guided Tulley's hand upward until she closed it over Sue's small breast. She kneaded the firm mounds briefly before turning her attention to the ever-lengthening nipple. Tulley rolled it roughly between her thumb and forefinger while Sue moaned into her mouth.

It didn't take long before Sue was arching her hips with every twist of her nipple, begging Tulley for more. Tulley slowly moved her hand down Sue's body until she could slide her fingertips just inside the waistband of the bottoms of the baby doll.

Sue quickly replaced Tulley's hand on her breast with her own. She teased both nipples as Tulley teased her. She flicked them lightly and pinched them hard, with Tulley watching the whole time.

"Tulley, please."

"What?" Tulley moved between Sue's legs. She peeled the bottoms off and followed their path with kisses as she did. When they were completely off, she kissed up the other leg until she reached the spot where Sue's legs came together. She kissed her pussy as passionately as she had kissed her mouth, her tongue delving deep and circling before delving deep again. She placed Sue's knees over her shoulders and glanced up to see Sue's eyes closed, her fingers frantically working her nipples.

Tulley dragged her tongue along the length of Sue, starting at her wet pussy, lapping through her swollen lips and licking from the base of her hardened clit to the tip. She circled the sensitive area, feeling it grow with every pass. She finally licked directly on it, sending Sue into gyrations against her.

Tulley continued her ministrations, each lick harder than the last, matching Sue's bucks against her. She lowered a shoulder and freed a hand to slide three fingers deep inside and was rewarded with more writhing and grinding from Sue.

"Please, Tulley. Oh, dear God. That feels good. Suck me, baby. Suck me off, please!"

Tulley knew that's all it would take. She sucked Sue's clit and lapped at the tip of it while continuing to thrust her fingers deeper and deeper.

Sue stopped all movement and screamed Tulley's name, her hot, wet pussy closing around Tulley's fingers over and over again.

When they were breathing normally again, Sue stood and pulled Tulley up with her. She kissed Tulley's neck while she deftly unbuttoned and unzipped her shorts. Tulley stepped out of them and her boxers while they worked together to unclothe first her top half, then Sue's.

Sue took Tulley by the hand and led her into the bathroom. She opened the door to turn the shower on, then pulled Tulley in with her.

They kissed anew as they lathered each other up, spreading suds over every inch. Sue moved her hand between Tulley's legs and combined the slick soap with the juices she was already creating. Her finger glided easily over Tulley's engorged clit and into her waiting pussy.

Tulley fell back against the wall and spread her legs wider. She groaned in appreciation as Sue's fingers slid deeper. Sue turned Tulley around so her chest was against the wall and slid her thumb inside her while her fingers played on her clit. It took no time at all for Tulley to cry out as she climaxed, then she fell back against Sue.

Once they were dried off, they lay together and dozed briefly. While Tulley slept, Sue went to the kitchen and got some grapes and cheese from the refrigerator and put them on paper plates. She woke Tulley by rubbing a cold grape against her lips.

Tulley sucked it into her mouth. "Do you have anything else I can suck on?"

Sue propped herself over Tulley and lowered a nipple for her to take into her mouth. Tulley continued to suck as Sue moved against her leg, finally collapsing in a satiated pile on top of her.

"I'm liking this staying in a hotel thing," Tulley said.

"If the rest of the weekend is like today, I'll never walk again."

"I won't complain." Tulley rolled over and positioned her knee between Sue's legs again.

"No more," Sue protested. "I need some sleep. It's not like this is a one-shot deal. We have the room all day tomorrow, too."

❖

Sue woke the next morning to Tulley's mouth on her nipples and her hand between her legs.

"Mm. Good morning to me."

Tulley looked up with a nipple between her teeth and smiled.

"Oh, please," Sue said. "Don't let me interrupt."

Tulley closed her eyes and ran her tongue over Sue's nipple. Sue watched Tulley's expression and couldn't get over the sheer pleasure written all over her face. She was certain her face was registering a fair amount of pleasure as well as Tulley's tongue flicked and teased while her fingers stroked along Sue's pussy.

Sue took Tulley's hand and pressed her fingers inside her, then moved her own fingers over her begging clit. She arched her hips to take Tulley deeper while she rubbed herself faster and pressed harder.

Tulley sucked hard on a nipple as she stroked Sue's sensitive spot deep inside. The combination catapulted Sue into orbit. She continued to frantically work her fingers over her clit to extend the powerful climax.

When she was finally back to reality, she coated her nipples with the remnants of her orgasm and watched Tulley greedily lick them clean.

Tulley kissed down Sue's stomach as she started to move her fingers inside her again. She ran her tongue over Sue's clit, causing it to slip out from under its hood. She licked wide swaths across it with a flat tongue while she slowly withdrew her hand before sliding it back in.

"Oh fuck, baby," Sue moaned. "Oh, God, you feel good."

She reached down and held Tulley's head in place with one hand, while her free hand tugged and twisted an erect nipple. She raised off the bed and ground her clit into Tulley's mouth. Tulley closed her mouth around it, causing Sue to press her face harder into her. Sue kept the pressure on the back of Tulley's head as Tulley continued to plunge her fingers deeper inside her, stroking the depths of her pussy as her tongue flicked across her throbbing clit.

Sue felt every muscle tense up as the orgasm started at her core and spread throughout her body. Her whole body trembled with the force of the climax and when she relaxed, she realized she had Tulley's head clasped firmly between her thighs.

"Sorry about that," she breathed. "Oh, dear God, that was amazing."

Tulley slid out from between Sue's legs and moved up her body, trailing kisses as she went. She finally lowered her mouth to Sue's and kissed her. Sue groaned into Tulley's mouth as Tulley's tongue continued its playful movements. Tulley finally rolled off her and lay next to her, running her hand over Sue.

"I like waking up with you," Tulley said.

"Me, too. I very much enjoyed the way you woke me up this morning."

"I could get used to that."

"Unfortunately, hotels aren't cheap, so this will have to be a once in a while thing."

Tulley looked at Sue, her expression one of sadness.

"What?" Sue asked.

"Nothing." Tulley rolled away.

"Don't do that, Tulley. Don't ever just say, 'nothing.' You need to tell me what I've done when I upset you."

Tulley took a deep breath and flung her arm over her eyes.

"What?" Sue persisted. "What did I do?"

"I'm telling you how much I'm enjoying this and your response is essentially telling me not to get used to it. Thanks."

"That's not what I meant. I meant this is wonderful. And I'm sorry every day can't be like this."

"That's what I was trying to say."

Sue propped herself up and pulled Tulley's arm away, so she could see her eyes.

"You need to calm down, sweetheart. You tend to overreact."

Tulley just stared back, not responding.

"I'm not criticizing you. I'm just asking you not to react so strongly without stopping to think and try to understand what it is I'm saying to you."

Tulley nodded and Sue got out of bed.

"Come on. Let's hit the shower then get dressed so we can go get some breakfast."

They wanted to be sure they wouldn't run into anyone they knew, so Sue drove them up into the foothills. They stopped at a roadside diner. As they got out of the car, Tulley took a deep breath of the chilly fall morning.

"It's gorgeous up here," she said.

"Have you never been up Highway Thirty-six before?"

"Never. Remember, I didn't do much except study last year."

"I plan to help you discover so much."

"You already have." Tulley blushed.

Tulley looked around and took in the rustic setting.

"It's so weird. All these pine trees make me feel like I'm a million miles away from Fenton, instead of twenty."

"We'll drive around and look at things after breakfast. But for now, I'm famished."

They entered the log building and a matronly hostess, with a bun of gray hair showed them to a booth.

"I wonder if they serve many lesbians here," Tulley whispered.

"That's an odd statement."

"Don't you ever think about that? Like how these people would feel if they knew?"

Sue set her menu down and leveled her gaze on Tulley.

"Do you think there's something wrong with being gay?"

"That wouldn't make sense, would it?"

"Not really. But that doesn't mean you don't feel that way."

Tulley's stomach knotted. She wasn't sure why, but Sue was making her very uncomfortable. She searched for an answer. Did she feel there was something wrong with her?

"I don't have anything against homosexuality. Obviously."

"Tulley, this is all still very new for you. It's okay to be confused and conflicted."

"What's to be confused about? I enjoy spending time with you." She lowered her voice. "I love sex with you. So where's the conflict?"

Tulley picked up her menu and pretended to study it, when in fact she just needed some protection from Sue's scrutiny.

The waitress brought their coffees and took their orders. With no menu to hide behind, Tulley was decidedly uncomfortable again.

"I really feel like this is important for us to talk about," Sue said.

"I don't know why. I don't deny who I am, if that's what you're asking."

"You don't?"

"Not at all. Would I be here if I did?"

Sue poured cream in her coffee and stirred it slowly. She looked up at Tulley.

"What about to everyone else?"

Tulley looked away from Sue. She stared out the windows at the hills of pine trees. All was still and peaceful out there. She wished she could feel half that calm. The truth was, she wasn't ready to come out to people. She lived in fear someone would find out. If she told Sue that, would Sue still want to see her?

"You said yourself," she finally said, "that you could get in trouble if people found out about us. Like people would think you were abusing your authority or something."

Sue stared at her and Tulley felt as though she could see right through her.

"Telling people you're a lesbian doesn't mean you have to tell them about us."

"Anyone I'd tell would know."

"That could be true." Sue smiled. "I'm not judging you, babe. I'm just trying to make you think. Would I like you to be completely out? Sure. Can anyone make you come out before you're ready? Not really."

Tulley was getting more upset by the minute. Sue wanted her to be out. She'd said it. Tulley felt like this was the breaking point. Sue'd given her an ultimatum. So this was how it would end. Sue was going to break up with her. She fought back tears.

"Baby? What's wrong?" Sue reached for her hand, which Tulley immediately pulled away as the waitress approached with their food.

The waitress walked off and Tulley stared at her plate, too upset to eat.

"Tulley? Say something. What's going on?"

Tulley just shook her head, not trusting her voice.

"Remember what we talked about? You need to tell me what you're thinking and feeling. I don't have any idea what I've done to upset you. Please."

"You don't know what you've done? You're dumping me. You didn't think that might upset me?"

"Where did you get that? I swear, woman! I don't understand how your brain works."

"You said you want me to be out."

"I do. That doesn't mean I don't want to be with you if you're not. You really have a bad habit of reading things into my words. You need to not do that."

Tulley exhaled. "I thought you were telling me you didn't want to be with me."

"That's not even close to what I said. Relax, babe. I'm nowhere near through with you."

CHAPTER FOURTEEN

After breakfast, Sue drove further into the foothills and turned down a logging road.

"Are we allowed to be here?" Tulley asked.

"Of course."

They drove through the dense forest and finally emerged in a parking area. They parked their car away from the various trucks in the lot.

"Where are we?"

"We are in one of the prime fishing spots for rainbow trout in Northern California."

Sue got out and led Tulley down to a clear stream. Tulley could see fishermen along the bank in both directions. She stared at Sue, amused.

"You don't strike me as the fishing type."

"I love to fish. As a matter of fact, I used to carry my pole with me at all times."

"Why don't you anymore?"

Sue shrugged.

"No time, really."

"So, how does a girly-girl like you end up as a fisherwoman?"

Sue backed up and sat on a log. Tulley joined her.

"I used to go fishing with my grandpa all the time when I was a kid."

"Really? I see you more as the stay home and play with Barbies type."

Sue smiled wistfully.

"I didn't have a lot of dolls when I was a kid."

Tulley thought she heard a trace of sadness in Sue's voice.

"What was your childhood like?"

"We don't want to go there." Sue stood.

Tulley reached for Sue's hand and gently pulled her back down. She placed an arm around her shoulders.

"I'd like to hear about it. I don't know much about you."

Sue took a deep breath. "I don't know what you want to hear. It wasn't pleasant. My grandpa was the only thing that got me through it."

"I'm sorry."

Sue shrugged. "It was a long time ago."

"Not really."

"Okay, so maybe not, but it seems like it."

Tulley wanted to hear more. Her heart ached to think of a young Sue not very happy. She wanted to believe Sue's childhood had been as filled with love and laughter as her own.

"Did you live with your grandpa?"

"On weekends, I pretty much did. He'd pick me up early every Saturday morning and take me far away from my family. We'd go on adventures every weekend. He'd take me to the zoo or on a picnic. Or I'd help him on the farm. But our favorite times were when we'd go fishing." She smiled. "I used to look forward to opening day of fishing season the way most kids look forward to Christmas."

Tulley laughed. "That's just so funny."

"I know it's hard to believe, but I can bait a hook with the best of them. Grandpa always filleted the fish, though. He wouldn't let me use the sharp knife."

"What was your grandma like?"

"Oh, she was nice enough. Kind of strict and more uptight than Grandpa, but she would let me help her in the kitchen sometimes. She'd let me bake cookies and pies with her. And sometimes, if I'd been really good or if things at home were really bad, she'd let me help cook Grandpa a special dinner."

Tulley felt like she should let it drop, but she couldn't. She needed to know how bad things had gotten at Sue's home.

"Were your parents married or divorced?"

Sue sighed.

"They were technically married. But Dad left all the time. They never got divorced, but they were rarely together. Dad would usually show up drunk and use us all for punching bags, then drag Mom back to the back bedroom. He'd be gone when we woke the next day and we wouldn't see him for weeks. And there were times he stayed for a while, but those were few and far between."

Tulley pulled Sue close.

"I'm so sorry."

"Really, I'm over it."

"How can you be?"

"I don't know. It happened. I don't live with them anymore."

"Why did your mom put up with it?"

"I guess she loved him. She obviously didn't care about us."

"How many brothers and sisters do you have?"

"Two older brothers and an older sister. My dad used to fuck her, too."

"What?"

"Yeah. That's why Grandpa used to take me away. He wanted to protect me. I'm ten years younger than my sister, and my brothers are older than her. My one brother, Michael, used to stand up for me, but he ran away when he was sixteen and I haven't heard from him since."

"Why didn't your grandpa protect your brothers and sister, too?"

"I don't think he realized what was happening. I said something when I was four or five about Daddy taking her into the back room and Mom being mad. She was unusually mean to me when he did that. I think that's when my grandpa figured it out."

"Couldn't he have done something?"

"I suppose he could have. I don't know. Things were weird. Maybe he'd given up on them."

Tulley stared at the water and tried to digest the information. No wonder Sue went from one woman to another. She certainly didn't have a strong role model for how loving couples act. She took Sue's hand in hers and sat quietly.

"So tell me more about your family," Sue said.

"Well, my folks are really good people. Anyone from around there will tell you that. Mom and Dad got married right after high school. They'd been sweethearts since junior high. I have two older brothers. They live at home still and help with the vineyard. We're pretty tight. Dad runs the vineyard and Mom's a housewife. I basically grew up running around the vineyard, hanging with my brothers and the kids of some of the workers. Not a bad life really."

"I love the sound of your family. I used to dream of having one like yours."

"I'm really lucky," Tulley said, realizing for the first time how true that statement was.

Sue stood and brushed off her jeans.

"Come on. Let's walk around."

Tulley stood and followed Sue along the stream. When they reached a large stump, Sue turned away from the water and led Tulley into a stand of trees. Tulley was amazed at how the trees blocked out all the sounds around them. She couldn't hear the rushing stream or the birds crying. It was so peaceful. The smell of the trees added to the serenity. She felt much more at ease than she had all morning.

"This place is amazing," she said.

Sue turned to face her and grinned. She pinned Tulley against a tree and kissed her hard. She closed her hand on Tulley's breast while her tongue forced its way into her mouth.

Tulley's head spun at the intensity of the kiss. She wrapped her arms around Sue and pulled her against her. Her whole body trembled when she felt Sue's hand unbuttoning her jeans. When she slid the zipper down, Tulley arched her hips, every muscle needing to feel Sue's caress.

Sue put her hand down the back of Tulley's jeans and squeezed her ass. Tulley gasped at the feeling, but that was not where she wanted Sue's hand.

Sue brought her hand around and slipped it between Tulley's legs.

Tulley spread her legs as wide as she could in the confines of her jeans. She wanted to feel Sue deeper. She needed her further inside.

Sue used her free hand to lift Tulley's shirt and bra. She closed her mouth on Tulley's nipple, causing Tulley to cry out.

Tulley moved her hips in time with Sue's hand, careening closer and closer to the ultimate pleasure only Sue had ever given her. She felt Sue's thumb on her clit and that was all it took. She screamed loudly as she gave herself over to the orgasm. She continued to ride Sue's hand until the sensation ebbed.

"I think we should get back to the room," Sue said quietly.

"I don't think I'm going anywhere right now." Tulley fought to catch her breath.

"No?"

"I don't trust my legs."

Sue laughed then kissed Tulley again.

"You are so much fun."

When Tulley's legs felt less like rubber, they walked back to the car and drove to the hotel.

As soon as they were in their room, Tulley pulled Sue to her for a long, passionate kiss.

"Not so fast, stud. I bought you—well, us—a little something to play with."

Tulley sat and watched Sue walk to the dresser where she took a long, rectangular box from the top drawer. It looked like a poster box, only wider.

"What is it?"

"Open it."

Tulley opened the box and pulled out what appeared to be a soft, black jockstrap with a dildo stuck in it.

"What's this?"

"It's called a strap-on. Here." Sue helped Tulley out of her jeans and boxers and slid the jockstrap up her legs. She helped her get the straps tightened comfortably.

Tulley stroked the dildo like it was her own cock.

"That looks really hot," Sue said. "Is it hitting you right?"

"Oh, yeah. But I think you're overdressed."

Sue quickly stripped out of her clothes and tossed them aside. As she continued to watch Tulley stroke her cock, she reached between her own legs. She stood there rubbing herself, her gaze on Tulley's hand.

"Lay back on the bed," Sue said.

Tulley did as she was instructed. The sight of Sue touching herself was getting her hotter by the minute. She wrapped her hand around her cock that was pointing straight up in anticipation.

Sue straddled Tulley just in front of the dildo and kissed her, her tongue immediately demanding entrance to Tulley's mouth. Tulley happily obliged as their tongues tangled together in their familiar dance.

Sue backed up and slowly lowered herself until the length of the dildo was buried inside her.

"Oh, dear God, that feels good," she breathed.

"Tell me about it. This is amazing. And you look so fucking hot."

Sue leaned forward and rested her hands on Tulley's shoulders. Using them as leverage, she moved herself up and down on the dildo, driving it deeper with every plunge, as well as pressing the other end into Tulley's clit.

Tulley took the opportunity to play with Sue's breasts dangling in front of her. It wasn't long before she couldn't take any more.

"Oh, jeez. I'm gonna lose it. Tell me you're close."

"I'm with you," Sue said. "Let 'er go."

Sue sank lower still on Tulley's cock and ground down on her hips. Tulley felt Sue's pussy sucking the dildo in deeper as she clenched around it when she came.

Tulley's orgasm hit at the exact moment Sue's did. She came hard, and soon it was impossible to tell whose come was whose as it all mingled on Tulley's thighs.

"Holy shit. We need to use this all the time."

"Easy, Turbo." Sue laughed. "Variety. It's all about variety."

"But that was amazing. Coming together. What a rush."

"That was pretty special," Sue said. "Maybe we should see if we can do that again."

She slid off the toy and lay on her back with her legs wide.

Tulley knelt between her legs and directed the toy at Sue's waiting pussy. She placed Sue's legs over her shoulders and drove her cock deep inside Sue. She slowly drew it out until just the tip of it was inside.

"Don't tease me, baby. Please. Give it to me."

Slowly, gently, Tulley slid the dildo all the way in again. With it in as deep as it could go, she softly thrust over and over, the sensations on her clit driving her mad.

"Come on, Tulley. Get rough. Fuck me hard. You know how I like it."

Tulley pulled out and then slammed back into Sue. She did it again. And again.

Sue arched her back to meet every thrust. Her head thrashed on the pillow.

"Go deeper, babe," she begged.

"I'm all the way in," Tulley plunged the toy as deep as she could get it.

"We'll have to buy a bigger dildo," Sue whispered before she crossed her feet behind Tulley and locked her in place as she cried out.

Tulley lost all thought and could only feel. Starting between her legs and rushing down the length of them until her toes curled, the climax gripped her to her very soul. She froze, orgasms wracking her body until she collapsed, spent, on top of Sue.

"I love our new toy," Tulley said as she nestled her head between Sue's breasts.

"Me too, baby. Me too."

Sue helped get the harness off Tulley and pulled the dildo out. She placed it between Tulley's legs and slid it inside her pussy.

"Oh yes," Tulley said, enjoying being filled. "But why didn't you just wear it like I did?"

"I don't strap on, sweetheart. But I'll fuck you with a toy. No problem there."

"That feels so fucking good," Tulley said as Sue slid the toy in to its base. She pulled it out then plunged it deep again.

"Oh God. That's amazing."

"I'm glad you like it."

Tulley bucked against the dildo, picking up speed to keep up with Sue, who kept fucking her faster and faster. Tulley felt like she would explode from the pounding her pussy was taking. She was teetering on the edge, but couldn't quite get there. She was panting, thrashing, praying for release, but it wouldn't come.

Until Sue finally leaned forward and ran her tongue across Tulley's clit. That was all it took. She felt her pussy closing around the toy again and again as she reached a powerful orgasm that shook her to her core.

CHAPTER FIFTEEN

Sunday morning, Sue propped herself up on her elbow and dragged a lazy finger around Tulley's nipple. She felt the areola pucker as her nipple stiffened. Tulley moaned in her sleep but didn't wake up.

Sue replaced her fingers with her mouth and slowly circled the nipple with her tongue before taking it in her mouth. She sucked it in deep as her tongue licked the length of it.

She smiled when she felt Tulley's fingers tangle in her hair.

She took Tulley's other nipple between her thumb and forefinger and twisted and pulled it while she continued to suck the first one.

Sue gave the nipple one last lick before kissing and nibbling her way down Tulley's stomach. She spread Tulley's legs and climbed between. Sue playfully blew on Tulley's hardened clit and watched her flinch. She lowered her mouth and licked the length of Tulley, feeling her clit pulsing against her tongue. She sucked hard on her, drawing it into her mouth.

She felt Tulley writhing against her, arching her back to force her clit deeper in Sue's mouth. Sue gave one more hard suck, then moved her mouth lower and buried her tongue far inside Tulley's wet pussy.

"Mmm," Sue murmured appreciatively at the musky flavor.

Tulley continued to move against Sue, her arches matching time with Sue's tongue. She reached her hand down and pressed her fingers into her slick clit. As Sue continued to fuck her with her tongue, Tulley rubbed her swollen nerve center frantically until a powerful climax racked her body, causing her to tremble from head to toe.

When the shaking finally ceased, Sue moved from between her legs to kiss Tulley hard on the mouth, sharing the taste of her orgasm with her.

Tulley reached over to the nightstand and took the strap-on out. "Now it's your turn."

"Oh, yes. I am so horny right now. I want you to fuck me hard and fast."

When Tulley had her equipment on, Sue got on her hands and knees. "Fuck my pussy from behind. Please…"

Tulley knelt behind Sue's shapely ass and shuddered in anticipation. She carefully guided her cock to Sue's waiting opening. She pressed the tip gently in, only to find Sue wet and ready. She slid her tool the rest of the way in, burying it to its base. Tulley pulled out until only the tip was still in, but Sue would have none of that. She backed up, taking the whole thing inside again.

Tulley could barely contain herself at seeing Sue this worked up. Nothing turned her on more than Sue's arousal. She began stroking in and out, faster and harder as Sue groaned her appreciation.

"I'm so close. So fucking close. Rub my clit, baby. I need you to get me off. Please, baby," Sue pleaded.

Tulley didn't break her rhythm as she reached around Sue and pressed her fingers into her swollen clit.

"Oh, dear God, you're huge."

"That feels so good. Rub hard, baby. I'm so gonna come."

Tulley did as she was instructed, her own clit throbbing and close to exploding as well. She rubbed Sue's clit as hard as she could, pressing it into her pelvis.

Sue moved back and forth on her hands and knees, forcing the cock deeper inside her, then pushing her clit harder into Tulley's fingers. She could feel the ball of heat forming in her core. She continued rocking, her mind blank, her body a giant mass of exposed nerves.

The ball inside her finally burst, shooting electricity throughout her body as her orgasm flowed over her. She was aware of nothing but the pulsing waves coursing through her.

❖

After their shower, Sue checked them out of the hotel and dropped Tulley off by campus to walk home so they wouldn't arrive at the house together. She hated having to hide from everyone, but she knew it was best for the time being. It wouldn't be like that forever. She knew that.

She was in a melancholy mood when she let herself in the back door. Her body was still on fire from all their lovemaking and she was filled with a soft glow thinking about it. Yet she couldn't help but feel sad at the fact that the weekend was over and she didn't know when they'd have another one like it.

She sat at the desk in her room and tried to focus on homework, her ears trained to the back door so she wouldn't miss Tulley getting home. Nothing she read sunk in and she was disappointed when the back door opened and closed and it wasn't Tulley.

When Tulley finally got home, Sue fought to keep an enormous smile from her face. It had only been a few minutes, but she was still extremely happy to see Tulley.

"Hey, you," she said as Tulley passed her room.

"Hey." Tulley leaned on the doorjamb, looking adorable in her jeans and flannel shirt.

Sue sought words, but came up empty. All she could do was stare at Tulley and fight the urge to pull her into her room and make love with her.

"What are you doing?" Tulley asked.

"Trying to study."

"Yeah, I should probably do that, too."

"I hope you have better luck than I've had."

"I doubt it, but I'll try. I'll see you later."

Sue felt empty after Tulley walked away. Her tiny room felt cramped and lonely after where they had spent their weekend.

She wanted to plan a repeat the next weekend, but knew it wasn't feasible. She didn't have the kind of money it would take to have secret rendezvous every weekend.

❖

The following day, as Sue was walking out of one of her classes, a notice on the corkboard caught her attention. One of her professors was advertising for a TA in one of his classes. It would be five days a week and the pay wasn't bad. Sue thought again of the wonderful weekend she'd spent with Tulley and thought how nice it would be to have a little extra money to make that happen more often.

She went down the hall to find Professor Montagne in his office. He looked up as she walked in.

"Hi, Sue. What can I do for you?"

"I saw your ad for a TA and I wondered what I needed to do to apply."

"Really? I have to tell you, I'm a bit surprised."

"Why?"

"You do excellent work. You're one of the department's top students. But you aren't very involved in the department outside of your studies."

"Well, I'm the RA at my sorority house and that keeps me pretty busy."

"Doing what?"

Sue realized how much she hid behind her job at the house. It wasn't that big of a responsibility and she knew it. There was no reason she hadn't been more involved at school. It was just a matter of wanting to finish up and move on.

"Just making sure things run smoothly."

"I see. I have to admit, I have limited knowledge of the workings of the Greek system. But it seems like your job would be more as a figurehead than anything."

Sue stared at him. She didn't honestly feel she owed him an explanation. She was a good student. He'd already said that. That was all the department should care about in her mind.

"The bottom line is, I'm thrilled to see you wanting a bigger role in the department, and I'd love to have you as my TA."

"Really? You had me worried."

"I apologize for that. But you are a mystery. However, whatever the reasoning for wanting to be a TA, it's my pleasure to have you helping me teach my class."

He handed her a syllabus for the class she was to help in, as well as a spare textbook.

"This is what you'll need to get started. It's Rec 101, which you took as a sophomore, so it will at least be familiar to you. Look over this stuff and meet me here tomorrow at two o'clock to set up a game plan."

Sue put the things in her messenger bag and was beaming as she walked to her next class. Things were looking up in her world. She hadn't felt this happy in years. If ever.

Tulley walked in after her day and saw Sue sitting at her desk in sweat pants and an oversized T-shirt. She was turned sideways in her chair, reading a book that was open on her lap. Her hair fell forward and blocked her face and Tulley fought the urge to brush it back and kiss her cheek.

"What are you so focused on?" She called from the doorway. Her heart skipped a beat when Sue looked up and their gazes met.

"Yet another paper for kinesiology."

"Sounds exciting."

"Not so much. Come on in. Have a seat. Tell me about your day."

Tulley sat on the bed and leaned against the wall.

"My day was okay. I spent the afternoon working with Gaby. That's gotten so old."

"You two sure put a lot of time into that presentation. It's not even due for a while yet, right?"

"Right. But it's interesting stuff we're researching, so I don't mind that part. It's the Gaby part."

Sue smiled and Tulley balled the bedspread in her hands, hoping that would keep her rooted in place.

"How was your day?" she asked, brazenly allowing her gaze to roam over Sue's curves, barely defined under her outfit.

"Whoa!" Danielle called from the door. "You look at her like that and then deny you two are involved?"

Tulley felt the color creep up her neck and cover her face.

"I don't know what you're talking about," she said defensively.

"Oh dear God, Tulley. You just stripped her and caressed her naked skin with your eyes. You can't deny it. I walked in at just the right time." She sat on the bed next to Tulley. "So now that the cat's out of the bag, why not kiss her for me? I enjoy seeing two women kiss. Not that I'm queer or anything. I just like it."

"I'm not going to kiss her," Tulley spat.

"Who's kissing who?" Kelly stopped in the hall outside Sue's door.

"No one's kissing anyone! Jesus!" Tulley bolted off the bed and squeezed past Kelly. She was fuming at herself. She couldn't believe she'd been so careless. She hoped against all hope Sue would convince Danielle she'd been mistaken. She couldn't take a chance on her sorority sisters knowing she was a lesbian. She dreaded running into Danielle or her cronies. The harassment would be unbearable.

She flung herself on her bed and fought the urge to cry. Her worst fears were being realized. She needed to get herself together, though. If they saw that they'd gotten to her, it would only be worse. She had to play it cool and never let them know that Danielle had, in fact, seen exactly what she said she did.

"So what the hell was that all about?" Kelly sat on the other bed.

"Oh, just Danielle being Danielle." Tulley hoped she sounded more relaxed than she felt. "I don't know why I let her push my buttons."

"What did she say? And what was that about a kiss?"

"I don't know. I guess because I was alone with Sue in her room, Danielle thought we were going to make out or something. Who knows what goes through her head?"

"Well, she sure managed to piss you off. You're right. You need to not let her get to you."

"It's just that I get so fucking tired of it. And it's always the same old thing. She's hell-bent on us being gay. And it's only us she bugs. Why can't she find someone else to pick on or at least pick a new topic?"

"Well, I think part of it is that Sue's never really hidden her sexuality."

"And I'm her friend so that makes me automatically gay? What? It's contagious or something?"

"Can I ask you something?"

Tulley's heart stopped. She didn't want to get into it with Kelly. She wasn't ready to come out and didn't want to have to lie to one of her best friends.

"What?" she finally said.

"What is it that you think is so wrong about being gay?"

Tulley flashed back to the conversation she'd had with Sue over breakfast two days before.

"Why do people think I have a problem with it? I don't. I'm just not."

"But so what if people think you are? Why is that the end of the world for you? What's the big deal?"

"It's not," Tulley lied. "It's Danielle that bugs me. She won't let it go. And it just gets old."

"I'm not convinced. I think maybe you need to figure out why you get so upset at the notion someone might think you're a lesbian." She stood. "I'm going to go watch TV. I'm glad you seem to be doing okay, anyway."

Tulley rolled onto her side and stared at the wall. She tried to climb deep inside herself to find out why she was so afraid that anyone find out she was gay. The first thing that came to mind was that maybe she wasn't, really. Maybe Sue was just someone to have fun with. But she knew, even as she thought it, that it was a lie. She had no interest in guys. She loved kissing Sue and making love to Sue. She craved Sue's touch in a way she'd never wanted a boy's.

She rolled onto her back and stared at the bunk above her, willing answers to appear. It didn't matter how she tried to imagine herself coming out to anyone in the house, her stomach knotted and she grew nauseated from fear. She wondered for a moment, if maybe the sorority was the problem. She considered that if she lived somewhere else, like Gaby, it would be easier to be out. People around campus seemed pretty accepting. They didn't have to deal with the constant scrutiny of uptight sorority sisters.

So the question was, did she move out and come out? Or stay where she was? If she decided to move out, she'd have to give her parents a reason. She couldn't come up with a plausible reason to give them. She could tell them she was miserable, which might work for her dad, but her mother wouldn't care.

She sighed. Her mother. Tulley's father loved her. Of that, she had no doubt. But her mother? That was a different story. Ever since she was a young girl, she'd been a disappointment to Diane Stephens. Her mother had been so excited to have a little girl she could dress up and treat as a little princess. It wasn't long before Tulley made it clear she was going to climb trees and splash in the mud with the boys, even when wearing frilly dresses and black patent leather shoes.

Tulley remembered being six years old when her dad brought home a pair of Wranglers for her. She had been ecstatic to have her own pair of blue jeans. She couldn't recall a loving moment with her mother from that point on.

She'd tried to make her mother proud by working hard at the vineyard and excelling in sports and getting good grades. She did everything she heard her parents tell her brothers to do. Still, her mother's approval eluded her. Tulley graduated from high school and went away to college, just as her mother had encouraged her brothers to do. They both chose to stay home and work, instead. Tulley had believed going to college might make her mother proud. But she'd been even more of an outcast her freshman year at Fenton than she'd been in high school. Since her mother placed such a level of importance on social graces, Tulley had only succeeded in disappointing her further.

Tulley's relationship with her mother had improved somewhat since she'd joined the sorority. She e-mailed her weekly with updates on goings on around the house and Thursday night socials. Her mother actually seemed happy to hear from her. So Tulley knew she wouldn't be able to tell her she wanted to move out of the house. She finally had a decent relationship with her that was tenuous at best. She didn't want to upset things. So she'd stay at the house and stay closeted.

She wondered briefly how her parents might take the news about her being a lesbian. She wasn't sure about her father, but was fairly certain her mother would never speak to her again. She couldn't risk that. And what if her mother turned her father against her? What if they disowned her? No, they must never find out, she decided.

Tulley climbed out of bed and headed to the game room. She needed to shoot some pool to relax and unwind.

❖

"I thought I'd find you here." Sue walked up behind Tulley, who spun so quickly she almost fell.

"What are you doing here?" Tulley asked.

"I came to make sure you're doing okay. Things got a little ugly earlier."

"You can't be in here alone with me." Tulley glanced at the door then back to Sue.

"Why not?" Sue laughed. "We're not doing anything."

"You think this is funny?"

"Tulley?" Sue realized Tulley was seriously on edge. "What's wrong?"

"What's wrong? Did you miss Danielle this afternoon? You know she's going to tell the whole fucking house. Pretty soon the whole town will know."

"Ease up there, Tulley. Think of it this way. At least we won't have to sneak around anymore."

"Are you kidding? Did you not convince her it was a figment of her imagination?"

"Sure, I tried. But, baby, you were pretty obvious. That look got me wet. It was hot and deliberate. And damned near impossible to explain away."

"Shit!" Tulley turned back to the table.

"Babe?" Sue crossed over and rubbed her back.

Tulley quickly pulled away.

"You can't touch me. What if someone walks by? And will you quit saying things like 'babe' and 'baby'? Someone might hear you."

Sue stepped back and swallowed the cold lump of dread creeping up inside her.

"Tulley? You're overreacting a bit, aren't you?"

"Overreacting? Danielle has the ability to ruin my life right now and you think I'm overreacting?"

"Ruin your life? Tulley, it's not the end of the world."

"So says you. Who cares if you're a lesbian? You're not close to your family. You don't care what they think. It's not like that for me."

"You're nineteen years old. Living away from home. It's high time you became your own person and quit worrying so damned much about what Mommy and Daddy think."

"Fuck you! You don't know anything about my parents. Or my relationship with them. Don't you dare try to give me advice on family."

Tulley's words cut deep. Sue had opened up about her childhood and told Tulley things she didn't share with many people. And now Tulley was throwing it back in her face. Sue understood that Tulley was scared. That made sense. But where had this hurtful hatred come from?

"I'm going to let you take that back." Sue struggled to remain calm.

"I'm not taking anything back. You don't get it. I'm not about to throw away my family. We love each other. I'm not going to hurt them."

"It seems to me if they loved you, they wouldn't care if you're gay."

"There you go again. Suddenly you're the expert on families? Bullshit."

Sue's hurt and anger were all-consuming. She felt betrayed by Tulley and didn't think she deserved that. She reminded herself that

Tulley was like a cornered animal and she needed to remember it was the fear speaking.

"Please don't bring up my family. I told you things in confidence, never dreaming you'd try to hurt me with them. I get that today was hard. But we need to talk calmly and rationally about it so we can move past this. Throwing insults back and forth isn't going to help anything."

"Move past this? You're kidding, right? You're crazy if you think I'm taking any more chances. There's no way."

"That's a pretty strong statement you just made. Why don't you sleep on it? We'll talk about it some more tomorrow."

"No! We won't talk about anything. I don't want to talk to you, see you, or have anything to do with you. You're not worth throwing my life away for."

Sue stood fighting tears as Tulley stormed past her on her way out of the room. She turned slowly and took a deep breath as she left the game room. Alone in her room, she closed her door and threw herself on her bed, finally allowing the tears to flow. She sobbed as she tried to absorb the fact that Tulley had just tossed her aside like she was nothing. She didn't want to believe Tulley's words. She told herself to give it some time. Surely, Tulley didn't mean that it was over.

Their weekend together had been magical. Sue replayed every moment of it. She was sure Tulley hadn't been acting. She was confident Tulley had been equally into her. Sue thought of all the time they'd spent together recently. She played back the hours of lovemaking. She struggled to grasp that Tulley could simply throw that all away. She couldn't believe Tulley could just walk away.

The tears flowed from the pain, the sorrow, and finally the anger. She was angry at Tulley for being so shallow and immature, but she was equally as mad at herself for daring to get close to someone. She knew how those things turned out. She had been a fool to think things with Tulley would end differently.

CHAPTER SIXTEEN

Tuesday morning Sue woke early, showered, and dressed, then took a cup of coffee to the front porch. Logic told her Tulley would more than likely exit the house through the front door, rather than risk seeing Sue. But Sue had thought long and hard the night before and realized she wasn't ready to let Tulley walk away. She intended to put up a fight.

She hoped Tulley had given some thought to things the night before, as well. She was fairly sure Tulley wouldn't seek her out, but maybe she would be feeling a little less terrified and a little more open to a meaningful dialogue. That was Sue's hope as she sat on the low wall that bordered the porch. She watched the rain and waited.

At seven thirty, the front door opened and startled Sue out of her revelry. She checked her watch, then turned to see Tulley standing, frozen, just outside the door.

"What are you doing here?" Tulley asked.

"Hoping to talk to you."

"I'm late for class."

"Not even close."

"You're sitting out in the rain waiting for me?" Tulley said.

"Yep."

"Did you not hear me last night?"

"I was hoping you'd have had a change of heart."

"Not likely."

"Tulley, do you realize how much you're hurting me?"

Tulley's shoulders drooped. She stared at the concrete at her feet.

"You don't need to talk to me now, I guess," Sue continued. "But I would like you to please think about what you're doing. You seem to think everything is so clear-cut and easy. You shut me out and life will be fine. But it's not that simple. You are who you are and you shouldn't deny yourself that."

Tulley kept her focus on the porch, not looking at Sue.

"And I don't want to believe that walking away from me is that easy for you. As much pain as I'm in, I have to believe you're in some, too."

Tulley leveled her gaze on Sue, her eyes like flint.

"Yeah, not so much. Now, I need to get to school."

Sue watched Tulley cross the yard and turn the corner. She took another sip of coffee, but it turned her stomach. She had to face the fact that Tulley wasn't interested in moving forward with their relationship. She wanted to crawl back into bed and stay there for the day, but knew she had to get to school, as well.

Sue walked into her professor's office at two o'clock, having spent the previous couple of hours trying to focus on the information he'd given her the day before.

"Do you have any questions about anything?" he asked.

"Not really."

"Good, then let's take a look at my lesson plan for the class."

They spent the next hour reviewing the plan. Sue made notes and asked questions until she was comfortable she could handle teaching the class in his absence. She would observe the next two classes, starting that afternoon, then teach Thursday's. She was looking forward to any excuse to be at school longer so she could avoid the house.

"Do you happen to know if any other TA positions are available?" Sue asked as she packed things into her messenger bag.

"I believe there are a couple more. But I'd hate to have you neglecting your studies, Sue."

"I'm not worried."

"What about your duties with the sorority?"

Sue recognized she was a walking contradiction from the day before.

"I think it's time I spent less time there and more time pursuing other interests."

"I have to say, I like to hear that. Although that's not what you were saying yesterday."

"I've given this a lot of thought. What you said yesterday really rang true. It's time for me to get more involved in the department."

"Excellent. Well, I think Professor Davis has some night classes she is going to want a TA for."

Sue's heart raced. Night classes would be great.

"That sounds good. I'll go talk to her now. I'll see you at five o'clock to observe your class."

She was light on her feet as she walked down the hall and found Professor Davis in her office. The professor was at her desk, wearing a black button down oxford shirt. Her dark hair was short, accentuating her square jaw. Sue had heard that Briana Davis was family, but hadn't paid much attention to her. As she stood in the doorway admiring her, she was certain the rumors were true. Rather than feel a longing for the woman, Sue could only think that was how Tulley would look in twenty years. She swallowed the lump in her throat and walked in.

Professor Davis looked up and arched an eyebrow at Sue.

Sue extended her hand.

"Professor Davis? I'm Sue Dobson."

The professor took Sue's hand in hers and smiled warmly.

"I don't know how we haven't met before."

"Me, neither."

"What can I do for you, Sue?"

"I understand you are looking for a TA for a couple of your night classes."

Professor Davis folded her hands on her desk.

"I am indeed. Although, I normally give those positions to former or current students of mine."

"Fair enough." Sue stood.

"Who's your advisor?"

"Dr. Bergstrom."

"I'll talk to him, get some feedback on you. Why don't you leave me your number and I'll get back to you?"

Sue wrote her name, number, and e-mail address on a sticky note and handed it to her. Their fingers met briefly and she was surprised at the smile on the professor's face.

"Thanks a lot." Sue left the office and went to the library, where she made herself study before her class with Professor Montagne.

Tulley got home from school and beelined it to her room. Kelly and Livie were sitting at their desks. She didn't say anything but sat at her desk and booted up her laptop.

"How was your day?" Livie asked.

"Fine. Why?"

"Just asking. Jeez."

"What?" Tulley demanded.

"Why are you in such a foul mood?" Kelly asked.

"I'm not. You two are just being weird."

"All I did was ask how your day went. You're the one getting all defensive."

"I'm not defensive."

"Suit yourself," Kelly said.

"Hey, it's dinner time. Let's get downstairs," Livie said.

"You two go ahead. I'm not hungry."

"I haven't seen Sue this afternoon," Kelly commented.

Tulley's insides turned. She just wanted to forget about Sue. And she wanted everyone else to forget their suspicions.

"What's that got to do with anything?" she asked.

"Just saying."

Livie and Kelly left and Tulley exhaled as she stared at her computer. She wondered how long she could avoid Sue. She was still angry Sue had been waiting to pounce as she left the house that morning. Why didn't she just let her get on with her life? Sue had been a mistake. She acknowledged and accepted that. But it was over and she wasn't going to be that stupid again. She longed for the day it was all a distant memory.

Her stomach growled and she remembered she hadn't eaten that day. She'd been very anxious that morning, so hadn't grabbed breakfast and hadn't bothered to take a break for lunch. She was suddenly starving and wasn't sure what to do. She wasn't about to take any chance of spending time with Sue, so dinner downstairs was out. But would she be able to get out the front door without seeing her? If Kelly was right and Sue wasn't home, she should be safe. She hurried down the stairs and out the front door.

It was cool and raining and she hadn't grabbed a jacket. She contemplated going back for one, but she didn't want to risk it. She pulled the hood of her hoodie up, shoved her hands in her pockets, and hurried down the street to Taco Bell.

She walked in and was shaking herself off when she heard her name. She turned to see one of the girls she'd met at the fair earlier that semester. She was with the lesbian organization. Tulley had no desire to interact with her, so she waved and turned away.

"Come over here, Tulley. There are some people I'd like you to meet."

Tulley struggled for an escape, but could come up with nothing. She took a deep breath and walked over to the table of young women.

"In case you don't remember, I'm Andrea," the vivacious blonde said. She pointed to the others at the table. "This is Miranda, Carly, and Delinda."

"How you doing?" Tulley managed.

"Pull up a chair."

"No, thanks. I need to get some food and get back to homework."

Tulley grew increasingly uneasy at the way the women were looking at her. Carly had spiky red hair and piercings on her eyebrow and lower lip. She seemed to be sizing up Tulley. Delinda had short brown hair and beautiful brown eyes. The smile never left her lips. Miranda was the only one who seemed to remember she had food.

"Okay. I just wanted you to know I've been really busy, but haven't forgotten about you. I still have your number," Andrea said.

Tulley searched her mind for a way to ask her to please lose her number, but couldn't come up with anything. She simply nodded.

"We're having a party Saturday night. You should come," Delinda said.

"Maybe I will."

"Or maybe you won't." Carly spoke up.

The others looked from Carly to Tulley and back. Tulley felt like she was going through some rite of passage, some other form of initiation that she wanted no part of. She shrugged.

"Maybe I won't," she said. "I don't know what I'm doing Saturday night."

"Or maybe you don't want to associate with us," Carly persisted.

"You all seem nice enough."

"So what's the problem? Are you coming to the party or not?"

"Carly," Andrea broke in. "What's with you? She doesn't have to make up her mind right now."

"I'm guessing she hasn't made up her mind about a lot of things." Carly turned back to her food.

The words stung Tulley. She bit back the words she wanted to say. She had made up her mind. She'd made up her mind to do the right thing and not potentially lose her family and all that was important to her.

"I've got to go." Tulley walked up to the counter and ordered her dinner, then left without another word to Andrea and her friends.

Kelly and Livie were back upstairs when she got home, drenched clear through. She stripped and changed, throwing her clothes over a rack in their closet.

"I thought you weren't hungry," Kelly said when Tulley sat back at her desk.

"I ended up getting hungry."

"Why didn't you just come downstairs?"

"I wanted to be alone. Is that a crime?"

"You know, I don't know what crawled up your ass, but I'd appreciate it if you'd quit being such a fucking bitch to us," Livie said. "We didn't do anything to you."

Tulley looked at her roommates, every muscle in her body tense for a fight, then realized Livie was right.

"I'm sorry," she said. "I don't know what's gotten into me, either."

"Are you still upset about yesterday?" Kelly asked.

"What about yesterday?" Tulley was defensive again.

"Danielle picking on you."

Tulley carefully weighed her words. She could admit to that upsetting her, but had to do so without confirming what Danielle had witnessed.

"Yeah, I guess I am. I'm really tired of her bullshit."

"We're not crazy about her either, you know," Livie said. "So please stop treating us like the enemies."

"I will. I'm sorry, guys."

They settled into their studies and Tulley was exhausted when they finally decided to turn off their light at eleven. She climbed into bed, but as soon as her head hit the pillow, her brain turned back on. Thoughts of Sue drifted through her mind. She closed her eyes tightly to try to banish the visions of the hurt look on Sue's face that morning on the porch. She fought to keep the memories of the weekend from flooding in. She tossed and turned, fighting to forget the challenging look on Carly's face at Taco Bell. She just wanted to forget about being gay. She didn't need to go to some party where everything would remind her. She needed to get away from it, to focus on her straight friends and doing the right thing. She fell into a restless sleep filled with nightmares of being chased and hunted.

❖

Sue was leaving class the following afternoon when she heard someone call her name. She turned to see Professor Davis hurrying to catch up to her. She admired the professor's outfit consisting of jeans with creases down the legs, a white oxford shirt, and a black blazer. She cut a very handsome figure.

"Do you have class right now?" Professor Davis asked.

"No. I was on my way to the library."

"Why not let me buy you coffee at the student union? I'd like to talk to you."

Sue stared at her, trying unsuccessfully to read anything in her expression.

"Sure. Coffee would be nice."

They walked across campus, enjoying the cool, clear autumn afternoon. The sunshine helped Sue's mood, and she felt more relaxed than she had since Monday. The cafeteria was close to empty when they arrived. Sue got them a table while Professor Davis got them coffee. She watched her approach and admired her confident gait. She gave herself permission to enjoy her time with an attractive woman. She didn't owe Tulley anything.

"What are you thinking?" Professor Davis handed Sue her coffee.

Sue felt the color creep to her cheeks.

"Nothing, really."

Professor Davis smiled, but said nothing as she took her seat across from Sue.

"So I spent some time with Rick Bergstrom after I talked to you yesterday."

Sue nodded and held her breath, unable to guess what to expect.

"He spoke very highly of you. I know your grades are stellar, but it was nice to talk to someone who's had a lot of interaction with you."

"I'm glad he had some nice things to say."

Professor Davis turned in her chair and crossed her legs. She picked an imaginary speck off her jeans, then deliberately reached for her coffee.

Sue fought to be patient, longing to hear what the verdict was. But she also grinned at the professor's obvious toying with her.

"Tell me why you want to be my TA." She focused her gaze on Sue, who squirmed under her scrutiny.

"Honestly?" Sue took a sip of her coffee to compose her thoughts.

"Honestly."

Sue pondered what the professor might want to hear. She needed to stay away from the sorority house and she wanted to make some money. She wondered which answer would get her the job.

"I'd like to generate a little extra income."

"Really?" She stared at Sue.

"Really." Sue tried to look nonchalant.

Professor Davis nodded slowly and took another sip.

"Fair enough."

"What was the right answer?"

The professor laughed.

"I don't know that there was a right answer. But I appreciate your honesty."

"So do I get the position?"

Professor Davis's gaze roamed over Sue's face. She nodded again.

"Yes. You do. And I'm very much looking forward to working with you."

"Thank you. You won't be disappointed."

"No. I'm quite certain I won't."

Sue sat quietly, trying to keep the sense of relief from showing on her face.

"Shall we discuss the lesson plan?"

"Yes, please."

Professor Davis reached into her briefcase and withdrew a syllabus and handed it to Sue. Then she took out a calendar and notebook. She moved to the chair next to Sue and proceeded to review the syllabus with her.

Sue fought to focus on what was being said, but she was too aware of how much the professor looked like an older version of Tulley. The ache in her heart over losing her had chosen a lousy time to flare up.

"Is everything okay?" Professor Davis asked.

Sue felt her face begin to burn. She was blushing deeply and there was no way to deny it. She'd been caught spacing out.

"I'm fine," she said weakly.

Professor Davis straightened and looked at Sue.

"I need to know you're serious about this. It's not too late for me to change my mind."

"I'm very serious," Sue said. "I'm sorry. I'll focus."

"Thank you. Now let's take it from the top."

CHAPTER SEVENTEEN

Tulley spent the next month submerged in her studies and immersed in sorority activities that didn't involve Sue. Aside from a few brief, awkward encounters, she had managed to mostly avoid Sue. She'd heard that Sue was TAing for a couple of classes, which kept her away from the house. Tulley was even comfortable joining her housemates for dinners downstairs. Sue had been to a couple meals, but was seldom around during the dinner hour.

As October drew to a close, the members of Gamma Alpha Epsilon got dressed up for their annual Halloween social with the Chi Lambda Taus. Tulley went as a zombie, complete with sickly white makeup and torn clothes. Livie and Kelly went as Sonny and Cher. The mood in the house was festive, and Tulley was allowing herself to enjoy her sisters and finding it easier to get along with everyone since she no longer felt like she was hiding a big secret.

They walked up the street to the fraternity house and found the expansive backyard had been covered and converted to a haunted house. They were each paired up with a member of the fraternity, who guided them through the dark enclosure.

"I'm Sean." A friendly looking, shaggy blond young man extended his hand to Tulley. "May I accompany you?"

Tulley laughed at the mad scientist costume Sean wore and shook his hand.

"I'm Tulley and yes, please."

"I've seen you around, Tulley."

"You have?"

"I have. I'm glad I get to pair up with you."

Tulley's heart stopped and the familiar panic kicked in. She cautioned herself to relax and have fun. And deep down, she knew she should be flattered that Sean knew who she was.

They walked in the opening of the haunted house and were greeted with black lights and men dressed as skeletons jumping out at them. One of them made Tulley jump so badly, she fell into Sean, whose arms were immediately around her for support.

"Are you okay?" he called into her ear above the cacophony of noise.

"Yeah." She nodded.

Before they left the front area, they were each given a shot glass of tequila. They quickly downed those and moved on down a narrow hallway. Suddenly, an arm reached out and grabbed Tulley, pulling her into a side area. Sean followed and there they were subjected to blindly running their hands over peeled grapes and cold noodles, meant to represent eyeballs and brains.

Tulley laughed at the juvenile presentation and was happy to get to the end of the table where more tequila was waiting. They did their shots and continued through the rest of the house, alternately being chased by chainsaw wielding crazies and werewolves and vampires.

By the time they exited the haunted house, they'd had six shots of tequila and Tulley was feeling no pain. She followed Sean to the keg and gladly accepted a beer. The music was upbeat and fun, and Tulley didn't hesitate when Sean pulled her onto the dance floor. She hadn't been that relaxed or had so much fun since her last weekend with Sue. She fought the momentary feeling of melancholy and let loose on the dance floor.

After several dances, Sean went to get them more beers and Kelly and Livie sidled up to Tulley.

"You sure seem to be having fun."

"I'm having a blast."

"What's that guy's name?"

"Sean. He's so sweet."

"He seems like it. And he's totally into you."

"Yeah, I think he is." She looked around. "Have you two met anyone?"

Livie shrugged.

"Not anyone in particular. Although that one vampire over there is hot."

Tulley looked around to see a tall, thin vampire watching them.

"He's not bad. You should ask him to dance."

"Maybe after another beer."

"You're such a chicken."

"I know, right?"

Sean was back with their beers. He looked at Livie and Kelly.

"Are you two having fun?"

"They are," Tulley said. "But Livie here wants to get with the Count over there."

"Really? Tommy? He's not a bad guy." Sean waved at the vampire, who smiled as he walked up.

"I'm going to kill you," Livie told Tulley.

"Oh, come on. Have some fun," Tulley said.

"Hi, Tommy," Sean said. "This is Tulley and these are her friends, whose names I don't know."

"I'm Kelly."

"I'm Livie."

"Very nice to meet you both." He never took his eyes off Livie.

"Well, we need to get back to dancing." Sean took Tulley's hand and led her back to the center of the crowd.

"That was so nice of you," Tulley said.

"He is a nice guy. I wouldn't have done it if he was a jerk."

"Really?" Tulley was surprised. She assumed all the guys helped each other get laid.

"Really. I'd hate to have anything to do with a friend of yours getting hurt."

Tulley beamed. She believed she'd found a guy she could really get into. Relief washed over her as she realized not all guys were jerks and she didn't need to be with a woman to have a good time.

"Don't you want to take a break?" Tulley asked, several songs later. She'd never known a man who liked to dance as much as Sean.

"Sure," Sean said. He took Tulley's hand and walked with her to the keg. He tried to fill her cup, but only foam came out. He dropped the tap and looked at Tulley. "Must be time to hit The Asylum."

They cut through the crowd, passing the word that the keg was dry. Slowly, but surely, most everyone meandered to the street to either walk or get a ride to the bar. Sean and Tulley ended up walking with a large group the few blocks, since the designated drivers' cars were full.

The group was loud and lively and the walk was quick. They arrived and joined their brothers and sisters at the long tables along the back wall. There was no more room for them to sit, so they stood leaning against the wall, talking. Tulley never wanted the night to end.

Someone put money in the jukebox and Sean asked Tulley if she wanted to dance.

"There's not really a dance floor here."

"So? Come on."

They found an open area and started dancing. At first, Tulley felt foolish, but soon other couples joined them and she once again found herself completely at ease. She didn't know how Sean did it, but he made her feel safe and happy. She wondered how she could let him know she wanted to see him again.

A slow song came on and Tulley pulled him to her. He laughed and tried to step back, but she was just inebriated enough to be insistent. He looked at her questioningly, but put his arms around her and held her while the beat pulsated through the floor.

When the dance ended, they stepped out into the cool night for some fresh air. They sat on a park bench in front of the bar.

"I'm having so much fun tonight," Tulley said.

"Me, too. I'm so glad I finally got to hang out with you."

"I swear you're like the nicest guy ever."

"Aw, thanks, Tulley. That's a sweet thing to say."

Tulley decided it was time to make sure he understood her feelings. She leaned in to kiss him. Their lips met briefly, the kiss soft and sweet.

"I didn't expect that," Sean said.

"You didn't?"

"Not at all."

"Why not?"

Sean took her hand and stared deeply into her eyes.

"I guess I just assumed you knew. Or would figure it out."

"Figure what out?"

"Tulley, I'm gay."

Tulley let her hand go limp in his.

"You're what?"

"Gay. You know, as in I like boys?"

"I know what gay means."

Sean laughed.

"I kind of thought you might."

"But how? I mean, you're in a fraternity."

"So?"

"Well, don't they harass you?"

He looked taken aback by the question.

"No. Why would they? Although, I'll admit I didn't come out until I was through pledging."

Tulley struggled to comprehend what Sean was saying. She'd never even considered there were gays in fraternities.

"I just can't imagine."

"It's not like I'm the only one."

"There are more in your fraternity?"

"Well, no, not mine. But there are quite a few gays and lesbians in the Greek system."

"I had no idea."

"Really?"

"What do you mean by quite a few?"

"Well, not tons. But maybe thirty or so throughout the system."

"Do your parents know?" Tulley blurted.

"About me? Or about the system?"

"Very funny. About you."

"No. I'm not out to them. Someday I will be, but I'm not ready for that and I don't think they are either."

"Don't you worry they'll disown you? That they'll never want to speak to you again?"

"Are you kidding? Why would I even think like that? I'm from a tight family, Tulley. My folks love all of us kids. They might not get it. But then, they might not even be surprised. I don't know. But I do know I'm just not ready to tell them. I'm guessing they'll be hurt, confused, maybe disappointed. And I'm not up for dealing with all that at this point in my life. But why would they disown me?"

"It happens."

"Maybe in the Dark Ages, it did. Or maybe with families whose parents are assholes. My family's not like that. I'm really lucky."

Tulley went back to the fact there were so many gays and lesbians in the Greek system.

"How do you know there are so many of you in fraternities and sororities?"

"We run into each other at functions."

"Functions?"

"Sure. There are queer functions all the time. It's nice to get together with others and just hang out."

"So you wouldn't care if someone from your fraternity knew you were at a queer function?"

"Why would I? I'm totally out. I can't deny who I am. Why would I choose to associate with a bunch of people who wanted me to?"

"It just seems…I don't know. I guess I'd worry about the judgment and rudeness and all that."

"There are people who don't like it, sure. But I don't worry about them. Those are the guys that find something wrong with everyone. I'm not crazy about them anyway, so why would I care how they feel about me?"

"That kind of makes sense."

"I think so. Hey, you want to go back inside now?"

"I think I want to head home."

"Oh, sure. Come on. I'll walk you."

They walked in silence most of the way, with Tulley lost in thought. She wished she could feel the way Sean did about everything. She wished she could be open and unafraid around her sorority sisters. And her parents.

"I still can't believe you'd hurt your parents like that," she finally said.

"As opposed to what?" he asked softly. "Hurting myself by living a lie? Or hurting some nice girl by acting like I'm into her just to keep up a charade? And how far do I let the charade go? Do I marry her? Have kids? And by then how many people have I hurt?"

Tulley thought his words made perfect sense. There were many, many people that could end up hurt by living a lie.

They got to the house and Tulley started laughing.

"What's so funny?"

"My roommates are totally going to give me grief for disappearing with you."

"Well, they'll be fine once you tell them I'm gay."

"You wouldn't mind if I told them?"

"Have you not been listening to me?" He laughed again. "I'm totally out up here. I couldn't care less who you told."

"Wow."

"I had a great time with you tonight, Tulley."

"Me, too. It's been fun."

"Can I enter my number in your phone?"

"Sure." She fished her cell out of her pocket.

"Text or call anytime. I'd love to spend more time with you." He handed it back to her.

"You might regret telling me that."

"I doubt it. Sometimes we all just need someone to talk with. I'd be happy to be that person for you."

She threw her arms around him and hugged him tight, feeling like she'd met a lifeline.

When the hug ended he kissed her cheek.

"Good night, Tulley."

"Good night, Sean."

She let herself into the house, her mind going a mile a minute.

❖

Tulley barely got through the next day of school. She was exhausted and contemplative. She dragged herself back to the sorority house by the middle of the afternoon and found Sean waiting on the front porch. Her outlook immediately brightened.

"What are you doing here?"

"I wanted to see how you were doing today."

"I'm wiped out." She laughed. "How are you?"

"About the same. I'll be happy to take you for a little hair of the dog. But I was wondering if you wanted to join me for a burger at O'Malley's."

"Oh, yum! I haven't had an O'Malley burger this semester."

"Well, then, come on." He got off the swing.

"I should put my bag away. Do you want to come in?"

"That's cool. I'll wait here."

Tulley opened the front door and almost barreled into Sue, who was walking out.

"Oh, hi, Sue," Tulley said easily as she let her walk past.

"Hello." Sue's response was cool.

Tulley didn't notice as she hurried up the stairs to deposit her backpack. She was too excited about spending time with her new friend. She felt so relaxed with him. She couldn't wait to spend a few more hours together.

"What's up with Sue?" Sean asked when she was back outside.

"What do you mean?"

"She sounded like a bitch to you."

Tulley paused to think. She realized that was the first time she'd seen Sue and not felt completely tense since they quit seeing each other. She tried to remember Sue's response, but honestly couldn't.

"Whatever," she said. "I didn't notice."

Sean shrugged.

"How do you know Sue?" Tulley asked.

"Everyone knows Sue."

"Really?" Tulley wondered if everyone also knew about her and Sue. "What exactly do they know about her?"

"What do you know about her? You tell me first." He laughed as they made their way toward downtown and O'Malley's.

"I think maybe I won't answer that." Tulley smiled.

"Fair enough. So did you make it to all your classes today?"

"I did. Did you?"

"All but my first one. I just couldn't get out of bed."

"Do you live in the house?" Tulley couldn't believe she hadn't asked him already.

"I do."

"What's that like?"

"How do you mean?"

"I mean, is it a constant party? Do you ever have time to study? Are there always strange girls coming and going?"

"Yes to all of the above. I never even try to study at the house, though. I do that on campus or at the Stonewall Center."

"The what?"

"It's a center for gays. It's not just for students, but that's mostly what you'll find there. We hang out, have coffee, do homework, whatever."

"So do you basically only hang out with other gay students?"

"Not only. But sometimes it's nice to get away from the heterodominant Greek system and just be myself."

They walked into the burger joint and got in line. There were four groups ahead of them. Tulley took the opportunity to ask Sean more questions.

"You're really okay with yourself, aren't you?" Tulley asked.

"You mean because I'm gay? Sure. Why not?"

Tulley glanced around as he said that. He cocked his head and stared at her.

"Wow. You don't like that word, do you?"

"What?" Tulley was embarrassed he'd seen her reaction.

"Gay. Listen, sweetie, most people around here don't have a problem with it. Sure, if you get too far away from campus, some of the locals tend to be a little more conservative. And of course, there are the farm boys. But most people around here don't give it a second thought."

They were at the counter and placed their orders. They grabbed their sodas and found a booth by a window.

"So, little sister, tell me what it is about being gay that you find so distasteful."

"I don't," Tulley fibbed. "I have no problem with you being gay."

Sean nodded sagely.

"And what about her?" He motioned to a tall waitress with an auburn ponytail clearing a table.

"What about her?"

"Do you care that she's a lesbian?"

"She is?" Tulley was shocked. "How do you know?"

He rolled his eyes.

"I know her. The point is, do you care? That she's queer?"

"Of course not. It's none of my business."

"It's not, huh?" He smiled.

"Not so much."

"Fair enough."

Another waitress brought their burgers and the conversation died briefly as they ate.

"Maybe you need to meet more gays and lesbians," Sean said.

Tulley was surprised to feel her stomach flutter at the thought. She was so used to dread and fear. But Sean made it seem like being gay wasn't such a big deal. It was just part of life to him. She found herself longing to be able to embrace herself that way.

Before she could answer, the lesbian waitress walked over and stood looking at her.

"Hey, Sean. Who's your friend?" she asked.

"Well, hello, Loretta. It's nice to see you, too." He laughed. "This is my friend, Tulley."

"What a pleasure." Loretta extended her hand.

Tulley took her hand, very aware of its soft warmth.

"Nice to meet you," she said.

"Are you new around here?" Loretta asked. "I would remember if I'd seen you before."

Tulley blushed at her bold stare, but refused to freak out.

"Not new, really. Just a bit of a hermit."

"Hermit, huh? Well, I hope you'll come out to play more."

Tulley smiled.

"I just might."

"Lucky us. I need to get back to work. It was nice meeting you." She started to walk off, then stopped and looked at Sean. "Oh, yeah. Good seeing you, hon."

Sean burst out laughing as Loretta walked off.

"What's so funny?" Tulley asked.

"Oh, come on. You're not that dense, are you?"

"I'm not dense at all. At least I don't think I am. But I don't know what you're laughing about."

"She was so obviously hitting on you."

"You know, I thought she was flirting."

"You *thought*? You mean you can't tell when someone is coming on? Even that strongly?"

Tulley shrugged, embarrassed, but secretly thrilled.

Sean leaned back against the booth and focused his gaze on Tulley.

"So did you tell your roommates?"

"Tell them what?"

"That I'm gay."

"Oh, no. I haven't seen them today. Well, briefly this morning, but then it was a mad rush to get to class on time. I'm sure we'll have that talk tonight."

"How do you think they'll take it?"

Tulley opened her mouth to answer, but then realized she didn't know. She thought for a moment.

"I don't think they'll care. I mean, they may be bummed because I think they thought I found a nice guy. But they won't really care."

"They want you to find a nice guy?"

"I think so. Sure."

"Is that what you want?"

"What do you mean?"

"It's a simple question, Tull. Is that what you want for yourself? To find a nice boy?"

Right battled with wrong deep inside her. Her struggle to move on and do the right thing had been her main focus for the past few weeks. Suddenly, she questioned what exactly the right thing was. She supposed she'd questioned it all along, no matter how she'd tried to convince herself she knew. But did she dare voice that?

"I'm not so sure." It was barely a whisper.

Sean burst into a huge smile. He slid out of the booth and pulled her to her feet, enveloping her in a giant hug.

"Good for you, Tulley."

She pulled away and looked him in the eye. She wanted to ask what he meant, to demand he explain his reaction. She wanted to clarify that he was mistaken. Instead, she pulled him to her once again and hung on for dear life.

"Come on." Sean finally pulled away. "Let's go to Stonewall and see who's there."

"I don't know…"

"Oh, come on. I just want you to meet some of my friends. No biggy. And if you get uncomfortable, we'll leave. I promise."

Tulley sensed he was sincere. She had nothing to fear. He would look out for her. She was comfortable and grateful that he seemed to want to ease her into this community. And she knew it wouldn't hurt to make new friends.

The Stonewall Center was two blocks away and was empty.

"Where is everyone?" Sean asked the middle-aged woman at the help desk.

"Honey, it's happy hour everywhere but here."

"True. Oh. This is my friend, Tulley. Tulley, this is Lauren. She helps run the place."

"Nice to meet you, Tulley." Lauren took Tulley's hand in both of hers. "Any friend of Sean's is a friend of mine."

"Thanks, Lauren. It's really nice meeting you, too."

"Well, I'll show Tulley around and then I guess we'll be on our way."

"Hey, don't forget about the faculty open house Sunday. Are you going?"

"Faculty open house?" Tulley asked.

"Yeah, there are several professors that are family. Every semester, one of them opens their house to gay and lesbian students. There are other faculty members there and usually a hundred or so students. It's fun and it's nice to feel a sense of community."

"I've never heard of it."

"It's not widely broadcast. But how about it? Would you like to go with?"

Tulley didn't hesitate at all. "I'd love to go."

"Excellent. Good food and good company. You'll like it. No booze, though. They draw the line at contributing to minors." He shrugged and smiled. "I guess we can't ask for everything."

CHAPTER EIGHTEEN

Sean walked Tulley back to the house and entered her number into his phone. He promised to text her and swore he wouldn't forget about taking her to the open house.

"Have a good day tomorrow," he said.

"You do the same."

"I'll be studying for midterms."

"Won't we all."

"See you Sunday, then." He started down the steps.

"Hey, Sean?"

"Yeah?" He turned to face her.

"Thank you. For everything."

"No problem, little sister. No problem at all."

She watched him walk off then climbed the stairs to her room. Livie and Kelly were lounging there, listening to music.

"Where have you been?" Kelly asked.

"Sean and I went downtown."

Livie turned the music down.

"Is that right? Do tell."

Tulley shrugged, unsure of how much to say. She wanted to tell them he was gay. She wanted to tell them she was gay. She wanted to shout out how free she felt. But without Sean, some of her courage wavered. It didn't disappear completely. But she second-guessed herself a little. Then it hit her. She wasn't afraid of coming out to them, but she felt she owed it to Sue to talk to her first. She needed to apologize to her and let her know her foolish fear was behind her.

"I promise I'll dish in just a minute. First of all, I need to talk to Sue."

Kelly and Livie exchanged curious glances. Kelly finally spoke.

"She's going to be in and out this weekend. I don't remember what she's doing, but she's not going to be around until Sunday night."

"Shit."

"Why?"

"I just need to talk to her."

"Is everything okay?" Kelly asked.

Tulley couldn't fight the smile. Even if Sue didn't forgive her and they didn't get back together, she knew Sue would be happy she was being true to herself.

"Everything is great."

"So let's hear about Sean. You two vanished into the night last night."

"We did." She threw herself on the bed. "Oh, you guys. He's the coolest person I've ever met."

"And you spent today together as well?"

"He was here when I got home from class. We went downtown for some burgers." She stopped before saying where else they'd gone.

"So?"

"So, what?" She tried to drag it out and make them crazy.

"Does our Tulley have a boyfriend?" Kelly asked.

Tulley burst out laughing.

"Nope. Not at all."

"But you're all grins and you two were so cute last night. If you're not ga-ga, what's going on?"

"Oh, guys. He's great. He's wonderful."

"And?" they said together.

"And he's gay."

"He is?" Livie looked stunned.

"Yep. Totally. But he's so much fun."

"I didn't think you liked gays," Kelly offered softly.

"So I was a close minded bigot."

"Well, I wouldn't go that far."

"I don't know. Not that it matters. It's all good now."

"What do you mean?" Livie asked. "You don't dislike gays anymore?"

Tulley laughed loudly.

"Oh, come on. You two can do better than that." She had no doubt they already knew. She knew they questioned her relationship with Sue.

"Oh, no you don't," Kelly said.

"No?"

"No. We're not saying anything. If you have something to tell us, spill it."

Tulley took a deep breath and steeled herself for their reaction. She knew she had to do this and felt the timing was right. Still, it was a huge step for her. She sat up on her bed and looked from one roommate to the other.

"I've decided not to deny it anymore. I'm a lesbian."

Kelly had her wrapped in her arms before she could think.

"I'm so happy for you. Congratulations."

"Congratulations?"

"Yes. You've done something remarkable by embracing who you are, by choosing not to live in fear and denial. I'm so proud of you."

❖

Sue was embracing her role as TA. At first, it was just a way to avoid Tulley. Then, it was an opportunity to spend time with Briana Davis. But she enjoyed interacting with her professors on another level. She didn't consider them her peers, by any stretch, but her relationship with them had certainly changed. She frequently had coffee or drinks with groups of them and discussed school, politics, or life in general.

Then there was the teaching itself. She enjoyed teaching. She was starting to wonder if perhaps a career in academia might be in her future. She'd always wanted to help run a Parks and Recreation district for a small town in Northern California, but her enjoyment of the hours she'd been spending in class, as well as preparing for class, couldn't be denied.

"Sue? Are you with us?" Professor Davis's voice cut into her thoughts.

They were at a small pub just off campus. A favorite of this group of faculty.

"I'm sorry. I was spacing out there. What did I miss?"

"Nothing important." Another professor smiled. "We just noticed you were a million miles away. Anything groundbreaking on your mind?"

"Not really. Just winding down after this week."

"Well, don't wind down too much," Professor Davis said. "We have a big weekend ahead of us."

Sue's stomach tightened. She had agreed to help the professor set her house up for a party she was having Sunday afternoon. She was planning on spending all day Saturday helping her set up. Professor Davis had made it somewhat apparent that she was interested in Sue. She flirted and touched, not inappropriately, but she usually managed some physical contact any time they were together, brushing against her, or making sure their hands met. And while Sue found her deliciously handsome, she wasn't interested. It confused her not to want to fall into bed with her. But something had changed after Tulley. Rather than throwing herself into meaningless sex again, she had completely withdrawn. She'd had such hope for things to work out with Tulley. And the promise of a true relationship had been so real. She thought she might still want that someday, rather than continuing a string of casual sex partners.

"I realize that. I'll be at your place at ten tomorrow," she finally said.

"Good."

Professor Bergstrom bought another round of beers and Sue sipped hers while she contemplated the weekend ahead of her. She left the pub a short while later and drove the few blocks to the house. She tossed her bag on her bed and grabbed some food from the kitchen.

She took the plate to her room and closed her door. She was feeling nostalgic and blamed it squarely on Tulley. Tulley had actually been nice that afternoon. She hadn't backed away from Sue at all when they'd bumped into each other. She'd been all smiles as she pushed past Sue to get into the house. Sue was sure she was up to something. Maybe she was seeing someone. The thought made her heart hurt.

She missed Tulley more than she cared to admit. Even a month later, she still did her best to avoid the house and, when there, avoided any contact with Tulley. It was too painful to see her. She knew Tulley had been hurting, too, but she'd climbed back into the closet and closed the door firmly behind her.

So why was she in such a great mood that afternoon? Had she woken up one morning over Sue for good? Sue decided she wasn't hungry after all. Depressed about Tulley and stressed over Professor Davis, she climbed into bed and lay there, waiting for her brain to shut down so she could sleep.

Sue woke the next morning, her mood not any better than it had been the night before. She had a knot in her stomach. While she admired what the professor was doing, she questioned why she had said she'd help. Still, she had given her word, so she showered and dressed in jeans and an old hoodie. She did her best to make herself as unattractive as possible.

She slipped out the back door and drove across town to Professor Davis's house. She lived in a nice two-story house in an upper middle class neighborhood that looked to have been developed in the forties. Sue drove past the cars lined up along the curb and parked three houses down. She walked back to the house, breathing in the crisp, autumn air. There was a note on the front door instructing her to go around to the side of the house.

Feeling even less comfortable, Sue crossed the driveway to the open gate and walked through it. She followed the walkway and the sound of voices around to the back of the house, where several people were standing around drinking coffee and talking.

"Sue, you made it." Professor Davis walked up to greet her. She wore faded Levi's and a long-sleeved dark blue Fenton State crewneck sweatshirt. Her baseball cap was black with a rainbow triangle. Sue thought she'd never looked better. She had to force herself to look away.

"Come on inside and we'll get you some coffee. There's doughnuts, too. Have you had breakfast?"

"No, but I'm fine, really."

"Don't be ridiculous. Come on in. I'll give you a quick tour of the house, too."

Sue searched for any excuse not to walk away from the crowd with the professor, but could come up with nothing. She followed her through the sliding glass door and into the dining room, which was covered with boxes of doughnuts and three caterer-sized pots of coffee.

"Wow, you know how to treat your volunteers," Sue said. She heard a noise and looked over the bar that separated the dining area from the kitchen. A woman was in the kitchen, looking in the refrigerator. All Sue could see was a very shapely ass in a pair of pink sweatpants.

"Hey, babe," Professor Davis said. "Come here. I want you to meet someone."

Sue's heart stopped briefly until she saw that the professor was speaking to the woman in the kitchen.

The woman straightened, her dark hair falling to her shoulders. She joined the women in the dining room.

Professor Davis put her arm around the woman's shoulders.

"Sue, this is my partner, Justine. Jus, this is Sue, the grad student I'm always talking about."

"It's so nice to finally meet you." Justine shook Sue's hand. "Briana speaks very highly of you."

"It's nice to meet you, too," Sue said enthusiastically. She felt the knot in her stomach melt. She didn't need to worry about

Professor Davis. She would be able to relax and do her duty, then leave. No worries.

"Well, help yourself. We have a lot of work to do today."

Sue grabbed a doughnut and filled a cup with coffee. She added some cream and glanced at the couple, who stood staring at her.

"What?" She was immediately self-conscious.

"Nothing." Professor Davis smiled. "Finish up. We need to get to work."

Something seemed off, but Sue wasn't going to obsess about it. She took her breakfast outside and surveyed the large backyard. The lawn was well manicured, with potted plants lined along the edges. There were long tables folded and leaning against the retaining walls.

Professor Davis came out and got everyone's attention.

"Thank you again to all of you for being here today. We really appreciate all your help. Our plan for the day is to split you into two groups. Most of you will work out here, moving plants around and setting up tables. A few of you will be brought inside to help us arrange things inside."

Sue stayed outside and was soon approached by a woman she didn't recognize.

"So how do you fit into the picture here?" the redhead asked.

"I'm a TA for Professor Davis. And you?"

"I'm in the history department."

Sue looked at her and couldn't decide if she was old enough to be a professor.

"My name's Lisa. And yes, I'm a teacher."

"You seem young."

"I'm not a professor. Just an instructor."

"I see."

"Come on, ladies. We have work to do." A man approached them. "Why don't you two start unfolding tables and getting them set up?"

Sue and Lisa walked to the tables and did as they were instructed. They unfolded a table, carried it to the markers on the grass, then covered them with butcher paper. It was a slow, tedious process to set up the fifteen tables. They had to weave in between people as well as plants that had been carried from the edges and placed strategically through the yard.

"This probably could have been planned a little better," Lisa said as she and Sue waited for two men to move with their planter.

"No kidding. Like maybe we should have put the tables out first." Sue laughed.

They continued to visit as they set things up, then helped the others get a giant tent top over the yard.

"This place looks great." Professor Davis stepped outside. "You guys did a great job. Now, how about some pizza and beer?"

Sue glanced at her watch and was shocked to see it was four o'clock.

"It was nice meeting you," Lisa said.

"Aren't you going for pizza?"

"No, I can't. I'll see you here tomorrow, though."

Sue was sorry to see her new friend drive off, but was smiling to herself as she drove to Rico's to join the others.

The evening progressed with lively conversation. Sue was tired and sore, but relaxed and happy. She'd made a new friend and that was always nice. A new friend was a great excuse to spend even less time at the sorority house. She ate pizza and drank beer and her heart felt lighter than it had in weeks.

Chapter Nineteen

Sue was up early Sunday, but moving slowly. She was sore from the manual labor the day before, but was looking forward to the day ahead of her. She would get to spend time with people she enjoyed, and while working behind the scenes, she still thought she'd probably get to meet some new people at the party.

The day was bright and sunny, so the first thing they did when she got to the professor's house was take down the tent. It was a cool morning, but temperatures were supposed to reach the low seventies. It was a perfect day for a garden party.

With the tent put away, everyone moved inside to help get appetizers made and put out. The barbecues were fired up and ready for hamburgers and hot dogs. Sue and Lisa joined the others in the den to watch some football while they waited for the guests to arrive.

Tulley woke Sunday with a smile on her face. She immediately sent a text to Sean, who told her he would be there at noon. He also reiterated how proud he was that she'd come out to her roommates and told her she should bring them with her.

"What are you doing again today?" Kelly leaned over the edge of her bed to see her.

"We're going to an open house at a faculty member's house. I don't know who it is. Apparently, this happens every semester. Do you want to go with?"

"Are you serious?"

"Of course. It should be fun. Lots of people. Mostly gays and lesbians, but you guys can totally go. And I'd love it if you did. I mean, I'll have a blast with Sean, but he's going to know all those other people and I don't want him to feel obligated to hang out with me."

"I doubt he'd feel obligated," Livie said.

"You know what I mean. But don't worry. I totally get it if you guys don't want to go. No worries."

"Actually, I think I'd really like to go," Kelly said.

"Me, too," Livie said.

"Really?"

"Sure. You're one of our best friends. We need to scope out the competition."

"Huh?"

"I'm teasing you," Kelly said. "But you're going to have all kinds of new friends now. You're totally expanding your social circle. That's a very good thing."

"Oh, I get it. Still, no one will take the place of you guys."

"Good answer."

❖

"They're here," Tulley said, slipping her phone back in her pocket.

Livie and Kelly followed her out to an early model Impala, idling by the curb. They slid in the backseat.

"Thanks so much for the ride," Tulley said to Loretta, the waitress from O'Malley's, who was behind the wheel.

"No problem. For you? Anything."

Tulley blushed but quickly recovered.

"These are my roommates, Kelly and Livie."

Loretta glanced at them in the rearview mirror.

"As long as neither of you has designs on Tulley, it's nice to meet you."

"No worries there." Kelly laughed.

"So you guys are straight sorority girls and you're going to a queer open house. That's pretty cool."

"Anything to support our friend."

"That's cool."

"Are you excited?" Sean turned in his seat to better see Tulley.

"I am! Totally. Thank you so much for inviting me."

"Oh, honey, we are going to do so much together. I can't wait to submerse you into your community."

"I can't wait."

"It's funny how little of this town I actually know," Kelly said as they headed past downtown and into residential areas.

"Fenton is a very quaint place," Loretta said. "There aren't many bad areas and there are some very nice ones."

"What's the area like that we'll be in today? Does anybody know?" Livie asked.

"It's not bad. It's an older, upscale neighborhood."

Tulley got more excited the closer they got. She didn't care if they were going to the poorest section of town. She was going to be with people like her. It would reinforce her decision to be out and reaffirm that she was still Tulley, just gay.

"How you doing?" Sean asked.

"Excited. Maybe a little nervous."

"Well, there's no need to be nervous, but I totally get that. These will all be new people to you. But it's not like rushing a sorority or anything. You're already a part of this group just by being you."

Tulley smiled at him.

"That's true, huh?"

"Yes, it is."

"Wow. Lots of people here already," Loretta said. "Do you guys want to get out while I go find a place to park?"

"We'll stay with you," Tulley said.

"You remember those words for later, you hear?" Loretta glanced at her in the mirror.

Tulley felt a slight discomfort, but chided herself that Loretta was just having fun with her. No one was that bold.

They found a parking spot the next block over and enjoyed the autumn sunshine as they walked to the house. There were balloons by the back gate, so they wandered that way and followed more balloons down the side yard until they arrived at a spacious backyard.

"This place is nice," Kelly said.

"Hi there." A handsome gentleman approached them. He appeared to be in his forties, dressed in khaki slacks and a pink golf shirt. "I'm Professor Hathaway. I'm in the English department."

"Is this your house?" Livie asked.

"No, not this year. I'm not due to host for another couple of years now."

They introduced themselves and made small talk before another group arrived and Professor Hathaway excused himself to greet them.

"There are some other Greeks," Sean said, leading them across the yard.

"Oh, joy," Loretta said.

"Don't hate," Sean cautioned her.

Loretta rolled her eyes and whispered in Tulley's ear. "Normally, I don't do Greeks, but for you, I'll make an exception."

"Tulley!" someone called.

She turned to see Gaby headed her way. She cringed inwardly. She hadn't even considered that she'd see her there.

Gaby wrapped her arms around Tulley and squeezed tight.

"Oh, my God! So you're out now?"

Tulley glanced around out of reflex, then remembered where she was.

"Yes. I'm out. Oh, Gaby. These are my roommates, Kelly and Livie."

"Hello," Gaby said coolly. "Roommates from the sorority?"

They nodded.

"And you're all queer?"

"We're not," Kelly said. "We're just here to support Tulley."

"Well, you two can go about your merry little ways. I'll take care of Tulley from here."

"We're not going anywhere," Livie said. "Tulley invited us so here we are."

"And that was nice of you, and I'm sure you get some sorority brownie points for rubbing elbows with the freaks, but you're not needed anymore."

"Gaby, don't you dare talk to my friends that way," Tulley said.

"What?"

"You're being a total bitch. Now, if you'll excuse us…"

Gaby grabbed her arm.

"You're not really letting them stay? This isn't for straights."

"What do you have against straight people?" Kelly demanded.

"It's more what straight people have against us," Gaby retorted.

"I have nothing against anyone. That's why I'm here. I can't believe I'm being discriminated against like this."

"Please."

"Hey, what's holding you up?" Loretta was at Tulley's side. "I thought you were right behind us."

"This person stopped us to talk," Kelly said. "We'll go with you now."

Loretta led them to where Sean was.

"Sweetie? What's wrong?" Sean asked, placing his arm around her and pulling her close.

"Is it that obvious?"

"Yes."

"We just met a total bitch," Kelly said.

"Anybody I know?" Sean looked at Loretta.

"I've never seen her before."

"She was bashing Kelly and Livie and telling them they didn't belong here."

"Why?"

"Because we're straight," Livie said.

"Hello, PFLAG, anyone?" Sean said. "I'm sorry. But let it go, because you're here to have fun."

Sean kept his arm around Tulley as he steered them through the group, introducing them to other Greeks. He proudly introduced her as a GAE, and introduced Kelly and Livie as straight, supportive friends.

Tulley soon relaxed and enjoyed talking to the others about their experiences. She was fascinated by every story about being out in a sorority or fraternity house. Most of them had positive things to say, but there were the understandable few bad situations. Still, Tulley was feeling more emboldened by the minute to come out to the house.

"Do you know where the restroom is?" Livie asked.

"Just go through the slider and down the hall. It's the first door on your right. You can't miss it."

"I'll go with," Tulley said.

"Me, too," Kelly joined in.

They were smiling and chatting as they walked through the back door, but Tulley stopped when she saw Sue in the kitchen.

Sue stared at her, a look of disgust on her face.

"What the fuck are you doing here?" she asked.

"Oh, my God, Sue." Tulley beamed. "I'm so happy to see you. I've been looking for you since Friday night."

"Why would you be looking for me?" Sue looked suspicious.

"We're just going to go on ahead," Kelly whispered, leaving Tulley alone to talk to Sue.

"Is there somewhere we can talk?" Tulley asked.

"Why? I thought your mission in life was to avoid me."

"Sue, please," Tulley said quietly. She'd been so excited to tell Sue of her newfound comfort in her own skin. She'd believed Sue would be happy for her. She hadn't expected such a cool reception.

"Please, what? Did you forget that you never want to have anything to do with me ever again?"

"I was scared."

"And I wasn't?"

"Not the way I was."

"Whatever. So what are you doing here? Aren't you worried someone might see you and tell your precious, holier-than-thou family?"

Tulley felt the tears threatening.

"I suppose I deserved that."

"Answer my question."

"Not here. I want to talk to you."

"Fine. Come on. Let's go to the office."

She led Tulley into a room with a brown leather couch along one wall and a desk that sat in front of the window. The trees right outside were varying colors of gold, red, and yellow. The other wall was covered in a panoramic picture of San Francisco Pride.

"What?" Sue crossed her arms and stared at Tulley.

"Can't we sit down or something?"

"Do whatever you want."

Tulley sat, hoping Sue would join her, but she didn't.

"Please sit down."

"Why? If you have something to say, say it and I'll get back to work."

"Sue, I'm really sorry for the way things went down with us."

Sue merely nodded.

"I was terrified. I panicked."

Sue unfolded her arms and slid her hands in her pockets.

"I thought if I tried hard enough, I could be straight. I could be normal. I could be the person everybody has always expected me to be."

"There you go again. Equating straight with normal."

"I'm trying to tell you what I was going through."

"Fine."

"But I don't feel that way anymore. I don't like hiding who I am. I'm not all alone in this world. There are lots of people who are gay, and they live their lives normally. They're not scared of everyone finding out."

Sue lowered herself onto the couch.

"And?"

"And I realized that sure, I'm scared of how my parents might respond. But no one's making me tell them right now. And living my life in fear, and denying who I am sucks. It's not living at all."

"And when did you come to these monumental decisions? And when were you going to tell me?"

"I told you. I've wanted to talk to you since Friday. That's when it was like someone hit me over the head with reality."

Sue leaned back against the couch and stared at the picture on the wall.

"So did you meet someone?"

"I did."

"I see. And you like her?"

"What? Her? No! Oh, no. I met a gay guy who helped me see what a fool I've been. We met Thursday night and then hung out Friday. And his happiness and openness was contagious."

"So that's why Sean was at the house."

"Exactly. He's been so awesome."

"I see. So what now?"

"What do you mean?"

"Well, for starters, you're here. So that's good."

"Did you see who I'm here with?"

"I didn't notice, to be honest."

"Kelly and Livie."

"No shit?" She broke into a wide smile. "So they know?"

"Yep. And now so do you. I mean, well, you already did, but you know what I mean."

"You know, Tulley, there are other kids here that are Greek. Word will get around."

"I know. I've already met some. It's all good. I'm determined to live out, loud and proud."

Sue pulled Tulley to her and held her tight.

"I'm so happy for you."

"Thanks."

Sue released Tulley and brushed a stray lock of hair from her eyes.

"I've missed you, Tulley."

"I've missed you, too."

"Have you? I mean, really?"

"Oh, yeah. I was just so confused. And so scared. But I'm sorry I hurt you. That sucked the most."

"Tell me."

"I'm so sorry."

Sue ran her hand over Tulley's forehead and down her cheek, until her fingertips brushed her lips.

Tulley shivered at the sensation.

"So how do I know it won't happen again?" Sue asked.

"Honestly? Every queer in the Greek system knows. I'll never be able to get back in that closet."

"I want to believe you."

"You should. I've never been more serious about anything in my life."

"And after college? Will you ever tell your parents?"

Tulley let out a nervous laugh.

"I'm sure I will. Someday. But for now, I just want to take this one day at a time and enjoy each and every day."

"That's a great idea," Sue whispered.

"Sue?"

"Yeah?"

"Are you going to kiss me?"

"Do you want me to?"

Tulley tangled her hand in Sue's hair and guided her mouth to hers. Their lips met softly, tentatively.

"I don't know, Tulley."

"What? What's not to know?"

"I don't know that I want to risk the pain again."

"What does your heart say?"

"I'm trying to listen to my brain."

"Don't. Stop thinking. Just feel."

She kissed Sue again and opened her mouth as Sue's tongue slipped inside. Tulley's own heart raced at the familiar tastes and feel of Sue's kiss. Sue kissed her deeper, laying her back on the couch and positioning herself on top.

"Oh shit, Tulley. I've missed you so much."

They continued to kiss, often frantically as the emotions threatened to consume them.

Tulley bent her leg, pressing her knee between Sue's. Sue responded by rubbing up and down along it, moaning in Tulley's mouth as she did.

"I don't ever want to be without you again," Tulley said.

"You won't, baby."

Tulley reached under Sue's sweatshirt and slid her hand inside her bra.

"Oh, dear God, I've missed your touch."

Tulley tugged and twisted the nipple and grinned as she felt it grow.

Sue climbed off her.

"Come on. We need to go someplace more private."

"Where?"

"Upstairs. No one has gone up there all day. I'm sure there are bedrooms up there."

Sue opened the door and poked her head out. Tulley followed close behind her as she darted out the door and down the hall then turned quickly up the stairs.

She pressed against Sue as they opened one door and found the master bedroom.

"No, not there," Tulley whispered.

Sue took her hand and they scurried down the hall to another closed door. It looked like a guest room, so Sue pulled Tulley in and locked the door behind them.

Tulley pulled Sue back into her arms and kissed her, falling back onto the bed. They kissed for an eternity before Sue got up and quickly undressed. Tulley lay back and watched, growing wetter by the minute.

"What are you doing? Get up and get naked," Sue said.

Tulley did as instructed and lay down on her side. Sue joined her and their hands roamed over each other as they kissed anew.

"I feel like I need to commit every inch of you to memory," Tulley said.

"Not necessary, babe. I'll never let you forget how my body feels. Never again."

Tulley moved her hand between Sue's legs and quickly entered her, easily sliding her fingers in deep. She was rewarded when she felt Sue's hand teasing her as well.

"Let me take care of you," Tulley whispered. "Let me please you first."

"I need you every bit as much as you need me," Sue said.

Their mouths met again, tongues mimicking the actions of their fingers. Tulley heard Sue's breathing quicken as she felt her own world start to teeter. She broke the kiss and looked into Sue's eyes.

Without blinking, she rubbed and plunged and pleased Sue, coaxing her onward and watching her fight to maintain focus as she bit her lip to keep from crying out at the same moment Tulley catapulted into oblivion, losing herself in the intensity of the moment.

"I love to watch you come," Tulley said.

"And I, you." Sue kissed her again.

"That was special."

"It was."

"No," Tulley persisted. "I mean that. It was different that time."

"It was right," Sue said. "It was right and it was beautiful. And it meant something."

"Did it not mean anything before?"

"Not like this time."

"So you felt it, too."

"I did." She rested her head on Tulley's shoulders. "Do you really not realize what just happened?"

"I guess not."

"We just truly gave ourselves to each other."

"Yeah. We did."

"So now you have me, Tulley. Please don't hurt me again."

"I won't, Sue. I'll never do anything that foolish again."

Sue kissed her and climbed off the bed again.

"We should probably get dressed and get back to the party."

"Oh, yeah."

Completely dressed, they hugged, simply holding each other for a few more moments.

"Are you ready?" Sue asked.

"I am."

Sue took Tulley's hand and held it tight as they walked out to join the crowd.

"Don't let go," Tulley whispered.

"Never."

About the Author

MJ Williamz was raised on California's Central Coast, which she still loves, but left at the age of seventeen in an attempt to further her education. She graduated from Chico State with a degree in business management. It was in Chico that MJ began to pursue her love of writing.

Now living in Portland, Oregon, MJ has made writing an integral part of her life. Since 2002, she's had over two dozen short stories accepted for publication, mostly erotica with a few romances thrown in for good measure. *Initiation by Desire* is MJ's third published novel.

Books Available from Bold Strokes Books

Worth the Risk by Karis Walsh. Investment analyst Jamie Callahan and Grand Prix show jumper Kaitlyn Brown are willing to risk it all in their careers—can they face a greater challenge and take a chance on love? (978-1-60282-587-1)

Bloody Claws by Winter Pennington. In the midst of aiding the police, Preternatural Private Investigator Kassandra Lyall finally finds herself at serious odds with Sheila Morris, the local werewolf pack's Alpha female, when Sheila abuses someone Kassandra has sworn to protect. (978-1-60282-588-8)

Awake Unto Me by Kathleen Knowles. In turn of the century San Francisco, two young women fight for love in a world where women are often invisible and passion is the privilege of the powerful. (978-1-60282-589-5)

Initiation by Desire by MJ Williamz. Jaded Sue and innocent Tulley find forbidden love and passion within the inhibiting confines of a sorority house filled with nosy sisters. (978-1-60282-590-1)

Toughskins by William Masswa. John and Bret are two twenty-something athletes who find that love can begin in the most unlikely of places, including a "mom and pop shop" wrestling league. (978-1-60282-591-8)

me@you.com by K.E. Payne. Is it possible to fall in love with someone you've never met? Imogen Summers thinks so because it's happened to her. (978-1-60282-592-5)

High Impact by Kim Baldwin. Thrill seeker Emery Lawson and Adventure Outfitter Pasha Dunn learn you can never truly appreciate what's important and what you're capable of until faced with a sudden and stark reminder of your own mortality. (978-1-60282-580-2)

Snowbound by Cari Hunter. "The policewoman got shot and she's bleeding everywhere. Get someone here in one hour or I'm going to put her out of her misery." It's an ultimatum that will forever change the lives of police officer Sam Lucas and Dr. Kate Myles. (978-1-60282-581-9)

Rescue Me by Julie Cannon. Tyler Logan reluctantly agrees to pose as the girlfriend of her in-the-closet gay BFF at his company's annual retreat, but she didn't count on falling for Kristin, the boss's wife. (978-1-60282-582-6)

Murder in the Irish Channel by Greg Herren. Chanse MacLeod investigates the disappearance of a female activist fighting the Archdiocese of New Orleans and a powerful real estate syndicate. (978-1-60282-584-0)

Franky Gets Real by Mel Bossa. A four day getaway. Five childhood friends. Five shattering confessions…and a forgotten love unearthed. (978-1-60282-585-7)

Riding the Rails: Locomotive Lust and Carnal Cabooses edited by Jerry Wheeler. Some of the hottest writers of gay erotica spin tales of Riding the Rails. (978-1-60282-586-4)

Sheltering Dunes by Radclyffe. The seventh in the award-winning Provincetown Tales. The pasts, presents, and futures of three women collide in a single moment that will alter all their lives forever. (978-1-60282-573-4)

Holy Rollers by Rob Byrnes. Partners in life and crime, Grant Lambert and Chase LaMarca assemble a team of gay and lesbian criminals to steal millions from a right-wing mega-church, but the gang's plans are complicated by an "ex-gay" conference, the FBI, and a corrupt reverend with his own plans for the cash. (978-1-60282-578-9)

History's Passion: Stories of Sex Before Stonewall edited by Richard Labonté. Four acclaimed erotic authors re-imagine the past…Welcome to the hidden queer history of men loving men not so very long—and centuries—ago. (978-1-60282-576-5)

Lucky Loser by Yolanda Wallace. Top tennis pros Sinjin Smythe and Laure Fortescue reach Wimbledon desperate to claim tennis's crown jewel, but will their feelings for each other get in the way? (978-1-60282-575-8)

Mystery of The Tempest: A Fisher Key Adventure by Sam Cameron. Twin brothers Denny and Steven Anderson love helping people and fighting crime alongside their sheriff dad on sun-drenched Fisher Key, Florida, but Denny doesn't dare tell anyone he's gay, and Steven has secrets of his own to keep. (978-1-60282-579-6)

Better Off Red: Vampire Sorority Sisters Book 1 by Rebekah Weatherspoon. Every sorority has its secrets, and college freshman Ginger Carmichael soon discovers that her pledge is more than a bond of sisterhood—it's a lifelong pact to serve six bloodthirsty demons with a lot more than nutritional needs. (978-1-60282-574-1)

Detours by Jeffrey Ricker. Joel Patterson is heading to Maine for his mother's funeral, and his high school friend Lincoln has invited himself along on the ride—and into Joel's bed—but when the ghost of Joel's mother joins the trip, the route is likely to be anything but straight. (978-1-60282-577-2)

Three Days by L.T. Marie. In a town like Vegas where anything can happen, Shawn and Dakota find that the stakes are love at all costs, and it's a gamble neither can afford to lose. (978-1-60282-569-7)

Swimming to Chicago by David-Matthew Barnes. As the lives of the adults around them unravel, high school students Alex and

Robby form an unbreakable bond, vowing to do anything to stay together—even if it means leaving everything behind. (978-1-60282-572-7)

Hostage Moon by AJ Quinn. Hunter Roswell thought she had left her past behind, until a serial killer begins stalking her. Can FBI profiler Sara Wilder help her find her connection to the killer before he strikes on blood moon? (978-1-60282-568-0)

Erotica Exotica: Tales of Sex, Magic, and the Supernatural edited by Richard Labonté. Today's top gay erotica authors offer sexual thrills and perverse arousal, spooky chills, and magical orgasms in these stories exploring arcane mystery, supernatural seduction, and sex that haunts in a manner both weird and wondrous. (978-1-60282-570-3)

Blue by Russ Gregory. Matt and Thatcher find themselves in the crosshairs of a psychotic killer stalking gay men in the streets of Austin, and only a 103-year-old nursing home resident holds the key to solving the murders—but can she give up her secrets in time to save them? (978-1-60282-571-0)

Balance of Forces: Toujours Ici by Ali Vali. Immortal Kendal Richoux's life began during the reign of Egypt's only female pharaoh, and history has taught her the dangers of getting too close to anyone who hasn't harnessed the power of time, but as she prepares for the most important battle of her long life, can she resist her attraction to Piper Marmande? (978-1-60282-567-3)

Wings: Subversive Gay Angel Erotica edited by Todd Gregory. A collection of powerfully written tales of passion and desire centered on the aching beauty of angels. (978-1-60282-565-9)

Contemporary Gay Romances by Felice Picano. These works of short fiction from legendary novelist and memoirist Felice Picano are as different from any standard "romances" as you can get, but they will linger in the mind and memory. (978-1-60282-639-7)

Pirate's Fortune: Supreme Constellations Book Four by Gun Brooke. Set against the backdrop of war, captured mercenary Weiss Kyakh is persuaded to work undercover with bio-android Madisyn Pimm, which foils her plans to escape, but kindles unexpected love. (978-1-60282-563-5)

Sex and Skateboards by Ashley Bartlett. Sex and skateboards and surfing on the California coast. What more could anyone want? Alden McKenna thinks that's all she needs, until she meets Weston Duvall. (978-1-60282-562-8)

http://www.boldstrokesbooks.com

Bold Strokes
BOOKS

victory
EDITIONS

Drama

LIBERTY
EDITION

AEROS

Mystery

C CRIME

Sci-fi

Sf
SPEC FIC

e-Books

HE
erotica

BSB
SOLILOQUY

BS
BOLD
STROKES
BOOKS

Erotica

Young
Adult

MATINEE BOOKS

Romance

WEBSTORE
PRINT AND EBOOKS